MURDER, *MURDER*

Mary Rita Marker

Mary Rita Marker

Llumina Press

ISBN: 978-1-59526-911-9

Printed in the United States of America by Llumina Press

Library of Congress Control Number: 2007907619

This book is dedicated to the memory of

Joseph and Helen Maxwell
my beloved parents

I wish to acknowledge my sincere gratitude to Pat Dorn of the Columbus Homicide Division for his invaluable help and to my editor, Linda Gorsuch.

Special thanks to my wonderful husband, Tim, for his support and encouragement throughout this project and to my sons, Patrick and Daniel, who have always believed in me.

and...Mickey

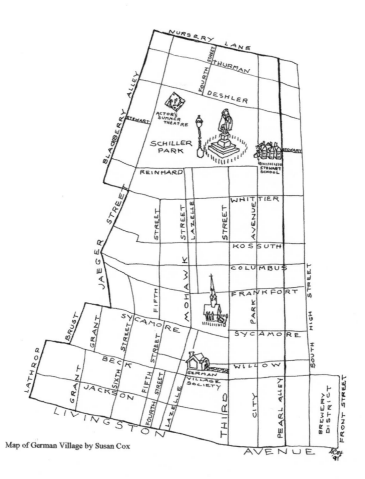

Map of German Village by Susan Cox

Chapter 1

Murder at Midnight
by Penelope Mitchell

It was a dark and stormy night. Fingers of sleet slid down the glass of the picture window. Miranda stood staring out into the darkness, her perfect profile illuminated by flashes of lightning. She had been without electricity and phone service for almost two hours.

"Oh, I wish he would come! Why doesn't he come?" All of a sudden, she sensed she was not alone. A whisper of danger...

"What is it, Tatters? I finally start my long-awaited novel and you have to go potty? Wait just a minute." Click and save.

Tatters whimpered yet again, so I took pity on him and let him out the back door. He quickly did his business, ran back to the house, and begged me with his big brown eyes to stay out a little longer. Unlike the weather in my novel, it was a beautiful June morning, bright and clear, with the smell of honeysuckle in the air. A perfect shorts and T-shirt day.

"You're right, Tatters. It's too nice to be chained to my computer. I've been at it a whole ten minutes and feel the need for a break. Thinking is hard work. Let's get your leash and take a walk in the park. Who knows? Maybe I'll find the inspiration to write the second para-

1

graph of 'The Great American Novel.' Let me slip on my sandals, and we're out of here."

Tatters is my adorable little ten pound bundle of joy. He is "Hollywood cute," with his blond head and gray-and-blond body. Tatters has floppy little ears that perk up when someone speaks to him, and he turns his head in an endearing way as he listens intently to every word. His bright little eyes are full of intelligence; sometimes I'm convinced he's smarter than most of the people I know. He doesn't like me to tell people that he is a Yorkie-poo (part Yorkie and part Poodle), so I tell everyone he is a miniature Irish Wolfhound. Funny thing is half the people believe me.

Tatters and I trotted over to Schiller Park, or at least went as fast as we could with Tatters stopping at every tree, bush, and lamppost along the way. I am grateful that Tatters is not a Greyhound racer. He would never cross the finish line because of all the pit stops along the way. Anyway, Schiller Park is a beautiful, twenty-two acre park in historic German Village, a neighborhood adjacent to downtown Columbus, Ohio. The park is only two blocks from my house, a charming, brick Queen Anne cottage built in 1897. I have lived in Columbus my entire life, and in German Village for the last eight years, since graduating from college. I really love the quaintness of the Village, with its worn brick streets and lovely wrought-iron fences and gates that showcase the brick and wood-frame houses. Homes, shops, and restaurants intermingle to create an enchanting atmosphere. The Village was settled during the latter part of the nineteenth century by German immigrants and is, I've been told, a cross between Georgetown and the French Quarter.

I parked myself on a bench and let Tatters sniff around. With his leash handle firmly under my foot, he could wander around a bit without getting into too much trouble. I could hear the church bells of St. Mary Church announce the eleven o'clock hour. My cell phone rang before I could get too comfortable.

"Buenos días, Penny. ¿Comment allez vous?"

"Oh, hi Mom. Why are you mixing your French and your Spanish?"

My mother, Angela, is an effervescent fifty-three-year-old pixie. She stands at five-feet nothing and weighs one hundred pounds soaking wet. Her chin-length, honey-blond hair and cornflower-blue eyes make her seem much younger than her years. Mom's current undertaking is learning Spanish. Last year she studied karate and knitting and, I have to admit, has become proficient at both. My mother was widowed ten years ago, and she deserves whatever happiness comes her way. She nursed my father through a long illness with cancer but, nonetheless, has maintained a positive attitude and a zest for life. She is an eternal optimist; heck, she's a Cubs fan! Mom's tribute to Dad is to live each day to the fullest. Mom always says that life doesn't happen to her — she happens to life.

"Oops! I hate it when I do that. It's hard to concentrate when I have so many things going on. Are you going to the shop today?"

"No, Mom. I've got it covered. I'm taking the day off to work on my book and spend some quality time with Tatters." My real job is managing a store called Whimsies, which I co-own with my mom's dear friend, Alice Dixon. Whimsies has an eclectic mix of merchandize, which we market with a dash of panache.

"If you are sitting at your computer slaving away, how come I can hear playground noises?"

"Well, I'm not actually working right now. I'm taking a break at the park," I replied sheepishly. I'll be thirty soon, but I still feel like a kid when I talk to Mom.

"Let me look out my window…yes, I can see you. I'll be right over. There's something I want to ask you."

Soon after my father died, my mom sold the family home in the suburbs, and she and my younger brother and sister moved to German Village into a grand, old, three-story Victorian facing the south side of the park. If I scooted down on the bench and squinted through the monkey bars, I could see Mom's house. I never get tired of looking at it. In my opinion, it's the loveliest house in the Village. It is a tall and stately red-brick Victorian with a charcoal-gray slate roof and a wrap-around front porch. The trim is cream and burgundy, which perfectly complements the brick. I especially love the turret on the left side of the house, which rises out of the foundation to touch the sky. A beautifully landscaped front garden is enclosed by an intricately-scrolled, black wrought-iron fence. When my father got sick, he and his partner sold their business and that, along with a generous life insurance policy and some wise investments, has enabled my mother to pursue her dreams and widen her horizons. She never tires of telling us kids that she is busy spending our inheritance.

Mom came out of the front door, locking it behind her. I saw her bounce down the steps and start across the street toward the park. Mom never walks; she bounces, skips, and flounces on nimble little feet. Today, she had on her favorite pink Capri pants with a checked pink-

and-white blouse and matching pink tennies. Mom has a sweet face with crater-sized dimples, which she uses often, and a kewpie-doll mouth. Many of the gentlemen in the neighborhood, old, young, and in-between, give her second and even third glances. She gave a little wave as she got closer.

"Oh, Penny, what a glorious day! How are you, sweetheart, and how's my little Tatters? You love it when I scratch behind your ears, don't you?" she said, while bending down to do just that. She was addressing Tatters, not me.

"Just fine, Mom."

"How is the book coming along?"

"Slowly, but surely. I feel that it's gaining momentum. What did you need to ask me?"

"The choir is performing at the Jeffersonville Outlet Mall today, so can your brother and sister have dinner with you? Alice (Mom's friend and my partner) is going with me to do some shopping while I sing." Mom recently joined a (formerly) all-black choir. After two years of voice lessons she still can't sing, but no one has the heart to tell her. She met the choir director at one of her gazillion committee meetings, and somehow convinced him to let her join the choir. No harm done. They stick her in the back in the baritone section to drown her out, and with the one-size-fits-all black satin robe, she can barely be seen.

"Sure, Mom. Taylor and Thomas are always welcome. Lannie is coming over after she cleans out her classroom, and I promised her a home-cooked spaghetti dinner to celebrate her summer vacation. There will be plenty for the twins. They can stay with me tonight if you won't be back until late." Taylor and Thomas, my baby sister and brother, had their last day of school yesterday. They will be sixteen next month, and just finished their sophomore year at Bradford Prep Academy.

"Oh, not to worry. I'll be home by eight. The next item, uh… remember the Village talent show that is coming up at the end of next week? Well, I had a couple all lined up to end the show with a fabulous Tango dance. They were a big hit last year. Anyway, the fellow sprained his ankle," she gave me a sideways glance, wet her lips, and continued, "and, the thing is, Penny, we need one more act to round out the show."

I looked at her with dawning horror. "You want *me* to be in the talent show? No way, Mom."

"But you have experience…"

"The only experience I have is a tap dance recital I was in when I was six and a piano recital I took part in when I was nine! I have definitely outgrown my tap shoes and, don't forget, at the piano recital I could only remember the beginning of the song. Everything else just went right out of my head, so I played the beginning twice and stopped. I was on stage for a total of twenty-five seconds!"

"Okay, okay. Just think about it. I have a few ideas… I would ask P.J., but he's going to be busy with the catering."

P.J. is my twin brother. He has a beautiful singing voice (inherited from my father), and actually considered singing professionally before deciding on culinary school. He is the executive chef at Bixby's-on-Broad, a fine dining restaurant with an upscale clientele located downtown. P.J. is very generous about donating his time to help out at the various Village functions. He lives in the north end of the Village on Sycamore Street with his wife, Grace, and toddler daughter, Lily.

Mom hesitated a minute, then continued. "Have you heard that Charley Walker is back in town? I was at Angles yesterday (our neighborhood hair salon that everyone laughingly refers to as 'Tangles') and heard that Charley came in last week for a haircut."

My jaw dropped. "Charley's back? No, I had no idea, and I don't think that Lannie knows either. I guess I'll have to tell her at dinner tonight. Do you know why he's back?"

"Haven't a clue. I was getting my nails done at the front of the shop, and I heard Stella say something about Charley while she was getting her hair shampooed in the back. Stella didn't see me, and I didn't want to go back and ask her because she would have told me it's none of my business. You know how Stella loves to have the upper hand."

Stella Morgan is a vindictive snot. She is mad because my mother did not use her as a real estate agent when she moved to the Village. The fact that Mom worked with my Aunt Lynne was not a mitigating circumstance, at least in her opinion. Stella is probably in her early forties and looks like a fashion model. She is tall and pencil-thin, with sleek blond hair and a plastic smile. She can be seen around the Village in stylish suits beautifully accessorized with broad-brimmed hats and stiletto heels. Not everyone could get away with that look, but, I grudgingly admit, she can carry it off.

"I have a manicure appointment with Janie this afternoon at two o'clock. I'll get the scoop before I see

Lannie tonight and let you know how she takes the news when you pick up the twins." I frowned. "Mom, do you think I should even tell Lannie that Charley's back?"

"If you don't, somebody else will. And that *somebody else* could be Stella."

"You've convinced me. Wish me luck."

"You've got it. On a lighter note, can I borrow your white shawl to wear to the dance on Saturday? If you're going to wear it, that's okay."

"Sure Mom, you can wear it. I think I'll wear my lavender sheath, and it has a matching sweater. You can pick up the shawl tonight. I'll put it out so I don't forget."

The Humanities League sponsors a benefit dance once a year for the missions overseas. The dance is held at Legion Hall downtown to accommodate the big crowd. It is family-oriented and lots of fun. Mom, of course, is on the committee, so we all go. P.J. and Grace have been busy preparing hors d'oeuvres for the buffet.

Mom slipped back on the bench and turned her face toward the sun. "It really is…whoa, Tatters, come back!"

Tatters took off like a shot, leash and all. I jumped up and ran after him, afraid that he would run into the street or that a bigger dog might consider him a tasty snack. He stopped at a garbage can, put his front paws down on the ground and rear-end in the air, tail wagging furiously. This is what he does when he wants to play. I saw the object of his attraction. One of those low-slung dogs, a Basset Hound I think, was tied to the lamppost behind the garbage can. The face looked somewhat familiar. Ah, yes… it looked just like Loretta Young, an actress who was famous during my grandmother's time. I love to watch old movies, and Loretta Young is one of my favorite actresses from the bygone days of cinema. She was classically beautiful, with a long face and gorgeous eyes. This particular animal bore only a superficial resemblance to the actress, but I was seeing it without makeup. The dog was just standing there, looking at Tatters. I bent down to pick up Tatters's leash and froze. A voice came from behind me that made my whole body tingle with just eight simple little words.

"Looks like love at first sight to me."

I don't know about "love at first sight," but it was definitely "love at first sound." That voice evoked a collage of images: picnics on a summer day, sailboats gliding across the water, and long, slow kisses. I turned my head slightly and stared straight into a...crotch. The crotch was wearing cut-off blue jeans that covered muscular, hairy legs. I could feel my cheeks flaming as I raised my eyes — the trip up was very good — taking in the rest. The chest was wearing a slightly damp, white T-shirt that stretched tightly over impressive pecs. I kept on going until I found the mouth that spoke those words. At that moment, those luscious lips were parted in a lopsided grin, showing white, straight teeth. My gaze kept on climbing, and I saw the most gorgeous green eyes ever made, set in a good-humored, handsome face. His dark brown hair had fallen over his left eyebrow, and his skin was a golden tan. He had one arm hooked around a basketball and the other extended to help me up. I graciously accepted the out-stretched hand and gave what I hoped was a dazzling smile. Thanks, Mom, for making me wear those braces!

"Hi, I'm Derek D'Amico. I thought Loretta would be okay here while I shot a few baskets. She usually just plops down and snoozes."

Ah, Loretta! I wasn't the only one who noticed the resemblance.

"Nice to meet you, Derek. I'm Penny Mitchell, and this is Tatters. He usually stays right by me, but, er, Loretta must be wearing some pretty special perfume today."

Tatters and Loretta started sniffing each other in that embarrassing way that dogs do. I had a fleeting thought of taking a sniff of Derek, but quickly repressed it. I desperately looked around for a distraction and spied my mother, still sitting on the bench, regarding us with a speculative look. I begged her with my eyes to come and rescue me. She obliged by hopping off the bench and heading our way.

"Derek, I'd like you to meet my mother, Angela Mitchell."

"Hi, Mrs. Mitchell…"

"Please, call me Angela."

"Well, then, Angela, I'm Derek D'Amico."

"Encantada." She flashed her dimples and offered her hand, which he graciously shook, raising a quizzical eyebrow at the Spanish. I hurriedly explained that Mom was trying to improve her communication skills in Spanish. I was secretly happy that she was learning to speak Spanish instead of taking up bull fighting. Derek seemed to accept my explanation and gave her a big grin.

"I have to skip along now, Penny. I'll talk to you later." She gave me a meaningful glance. "Nice meeting you, Derek." She started to leave, then turned back to ask, "Do you know about the benefit dance this coming Saturday night?"

Derek nodded and answered, "My real estate agent told me about it, and I am planning to go. It seems like a good way to meet my neighbors."

My mother beamed and then off she went.

"Your mother reminds me of the Energizer Bunny. Is she always that perky?"

"Always. Mom is sort of a cross between Albert Einstein and Mickey Mouse, not that she has frizzy hair and big ears, just that she's very bright and has a playful streak." We watched Mom cross the street and head toward home. "Mom lives right over there," I said, pointing to her house.

"Beautiful place! Do you live in the Village, Penny?"

"Yes. I live just a stone's throw from the park, over on Fifth Street. How about you?"

"I'm the new kid on the block. I'm redoing the vacant fruit market on Mohawk Street and converting it into a coffee shop. The carpenters are finishing up the living quarters over the shop as we speak. I've been staying at the Great Southern Hotel downtown and get to move into my new home tomorrow. I plan to open the shop early next week."

"You're Full of Beans!" I cried.

"Um…yes…well, that's the name of the shop. You know about it?"

I was referring to the new shop across the street from my own store. The various construction crews had been in and out for over a month getting the premises ready for business. I was totally delighted when I heard about

11

the new place several months ago, because it could only bring new business my way. I knew that the owner was a successful entrepreneur, but I had imagined someone much older. Derek looked to be in his early thirties.

"We really are neighbors. I co-own Whimsies, right across the street from you."

"I know the store. I've been in there and am really impressed with the setup." He gave me a genuine smile as I basked in his admiration. "I'd better go now. I needed to get away for a little while from all the flurry and noise. Hopefully, by now, the plumber and the tile layer will have settled their differences. I'm sure we'll be seeing lots of each other." He untied Loretta and gave me a little wave.

Ah, sigh, sigh. "Bye, Derek. See you soon."

"Tatters, YOU DA DOG!" I scratched his ears and hugged him. "I really should be mad at you for running away, but if you like Loretta as much I think I like Derek, I forgive you. Come on, let's go home, and I'll give you a treat." Tatters liked that suggestion.

I was content to let Tatters take the lead and zigzag the way home. I smiled as I replayed my encounter with Derek. Was he really as nice as he seemed? I guess I would have plenty of time to find out since he would be working and living so close to my shop. It had been a long time since I had a reaction like that. In fact, I don't think I've ever felt so strongly about someone right off the bat. Then, I remembered the conversation with Mom about Charley, and that brought me back to earth. I wondered again about Lannie's reaction to the news.

Lannie Daugherty (mother Ann and father Larry, need I say more?) has been my best friend since kindergarten. Her father moved their family to Columbus from Louisville when he joined my father's engineering firm. Our families share that special relationship in which the children call the other set of parents by their first names. Lannie and I know each other inside and out. It's liberating to have someone who knows me so well because we can forgo the social niceties and just enjoy being together. Larry and Ann moved to Florida after the sale of the firm. Mom and the kids go to visit them every year during Christmas break.

Lannie stayed in Columbus to go to college. She met Charley Walker during her last year at Ohio State and became infatuated with his good looks and outgoing manner. Charley is handsome; I'll give him that. He has a lean, athletic build, dark blond hair, and sky-blue eyes. Some say he has a confident manner — I call him cocky. I didn't like him from the moment I met him. Charley has never treated Lannie well. He was the master of "put downs," and would say things to Lannie like, "Those jeans make your ass look like the side of a barn," or, "Go get me another beer, babe."

I told Charley once that I didn't like the way he was treating Lannie, and he told me, "Butt out, sister, it's none of your business. Lannie likes the way I treat her just fine."

You get the idea. Anyway, Lannie and Charley got married right after graduation. I think she married him more for, "Oh, no, I'm graduating and I don't know what to do, so I'll get married" than for any real love for Charley. Her friends tried to act happy for her after we desperately tried to talk her out of it, and she sincerely tried to make a go of it. I didn't see her much after the marriage. Charley discouraged her from spending time with her old friends. She always said she was busy working on the house or preparing materials for her class (Lannie teaches junior English at North High School), to explain why she couldn't join us for the occasional night out. I knew better.

The straw that broke the camel's back was the punch that blackened Lannie's eye. Six months after marrying the creep, Lannie showed up on my doorstep with a suitcase. She looked broken — shrunken and defeated. The Lannie I know and love is beautiful. She is statuesque with rich auburn hair, mischievous amber eyes, a quick wit, and a smart mouth. This pitiful creature was a stranger. I called Mom, and we had an intervention with Lannie right then and there. I'll never forget my mother's face when she saw Lannie. Her mouth tightened and her blue eyes shot sparks of anger. Mom has always had a soft spot for Lannie. We talked late into the night and convinced her to save her life and leave Charley. Much to our dismay, Lannie refused to press charges against Charley because she sincerely liked his mother and did not want to humiliate her. She did, however, start divorce proceedings, and was legally a free woman by the one year anniversary of her wedding.

That was seven years ago. The road to recovery has been a difficult one for Lannie. It took a long time for her to regain her self-confidence and learn to trust people again. Lannie has not dated much over the years, I think because she is afraid of being hurt again. At least she is not bitter, nor does she harbor any ill feelings toward Charley.

About a year ago she told me, "You know, Penny, I feel sorry for Charley. He could have had all my love, but he threw it away. Thanks to him, I'm a stronger person than I ever thought I could be. At least I know I can love, but I don't think he can. The feelings he had for me were more of a sick obsession. He tried to insinuate himself into every aspect of my life and control my thoughts and actions. Charley needed me for his own ego; he didn't want me to grow and reach my potential. At the beginning, I think he admired my strength and, when I became his doormat, he became disgusted and tried to humiliate and debase me. I finally came to the conclusion that I was better than that and better off without him."

Tatters and I reached our front gate. I shook off my thoughts of Lannie and Charley and stood outside admiring the view for a minute before going in. My house is a one-and-a-half story Queen Anne cottage made of purplish-red brick. I moved here three years ago from a duplex on Lansing Street, a few blocks away, after the business starting taking off. I especially love my intricately-carved front door, painted purple, with its leaded-glass insert, and the arched front picture window in the parlor, with leaded glass in the upper portion of the arch. The glass catches the afternoon sunlight and sprays a rainbow of colors into the front rooms. The layout of my house is practical. The front door opens to a foyer large enough to hold a couple of pieces of furniture. To the left is my front parlor. Straight ahead from the foyer is a dining room, which can accommodate a table for eight. The ceilings in the downstairs rooms are ten feet tall, making the house appear more spacious than it actually is. Nestled between the dining room and parlor is my den, which can be closed off with pocket doors. I have my plasma TV, books, computer, and desk in the den, along with a loveseat and two comfortable chairs. A hallway from the dining room leads to a good-sized half bath and on to the kitchen. My kitchen is just large enough for a center island with seating for two. There are oak wood floors, stained a rich honey, throughout the first floor that are original to the house. Directly off the kitchen, to the right, is a small laundry room with a stackable washer and dryer and, to the left, a little screened-in back porch. The upstairs consists of a master bedroom suite and a guest suite. These areas are carpeted to keep down the noise and for warmth. My color palette for the house is green, gold, and cranberry. The garage is off the back of the house, accessible from the alley. Parking spaces are at a premium in German Village, so I'm very lucky to have a garage. The Village is only about one square mile in size and pedestrian friendly, so I rarely have to use my car.

I glanced at my watch and gave a little gasp of surprise. It was almost noon, and I wanted to write a little before my two o'clock appointment at Angles. I fixed myself a PBJ and sat down at the computer.

Chapter 2

Kevin removed his shoes, placing them on the mat by the front door. He knew there would be hell to pay if he muddied the polished marble foyer. Miranda was a meticulous housekeeper.

"Miranda, where are you?" he called softly, as he headed toward the kitchen. Kevin did not want to startle her. She would be nervous enough with the storm still raging. Miranda had always feared thunderstorms, and she had good reason to be terrified. Ever since...

"Time for me to go, Tatters. You be a good boy." I gave him a perfunctory pat on the head and myself a mental pat on the back for at least starting my book. I have wanted to be a writer ever since grade school. I loved losing myself in *Anne of Green Gables*, *Black Beauty*, and the *Nancy Drew* mystery series. My tastes evolved as I got older, but I have never lost the thrill and anticipation of starting a new book. My heart beats fast and my throat goes dry whenever a new Pat Conroy or Lillian Jackson Braun hits the shelves.

I deliberately left my house a little bit early to give myself time to stop at Whimsies before my appointment. Two blocks later, I rounded the corner and spotted the sign for Angles. My eye traveled past the sign and the two houses to the right of it. The next building is Whimsies, which has served as various establishments over the last hundred years: meat market, flower shop, card store, bakery, and family home. It is a narrow and deep wood-framed building, painted gray-blue with white trim. Two huge, plate-glass windows adorn either side of the highly-varnished front door. **Whimsies** is written in big, bold letters across one of the windows. Beneath the windows are white flower boxes filled with brightly-colored petunias and geraniums. An old carriage stoop sits proudly on the curb in front of the store. I love the rich tradition of the Village, and sometimes when I close my eyes I feel as if I've gone back an entire century. Some places just have a special feeling.

"Hi Paula," I greeted, as I walked in the door. Paula was arranging some newly-arrived glassware in the display cabinet by the entrance. I like to put the prettiest pieces at the front to better entice the customers.

"Hey, Penny, business is hopping today." She nodded her head toward Andy, who was busy ringing up a sale. Cha-ching! Hurray.

Paula and Andy are a godsend. They love Whimsies as much as Alice and I do. They came to work for us soon after the shop opened, and have taken on more and more responsibility with each passing year. I trust them implicitly. Alice is almost semi-retired at this point, and I can now put in forty hours a week instead of the eighty hours I used to thanks to Paula and Andy. Paula has good instincts for marketing our merchandize and a keen eye for detail. Andy is just wonderful with the customers, making them feel welcome and at home. They have been married for over thirty years, and are starting to look like each other; stout, salt and pepper hair, broad features, bespectacled brown eyes, and ready smiles. Nothing ever ruffles them. They don't have children, so they tend to dote on me. I like that.

"I just wanted to check in to see how things are going."

"No problems today. Janie, from Angles, called a minute ago to try to catch you before your appointment. She must have just missed you at the house. Anyway, she said to tell you, if I saw you, that she's running about fifteen minutes late. She said something about an emergency…"

A *manicure* emergency?

"…and I saw Stella go by a few minutes ago." She gave me a knowing look.

Ah, Stella. That explains it. Probably a hangnail or some such disaster.

"That's okay. It gives me a little time to look over the latest delivery. Did the copper canister sets come in?"

"Uh huh. They are right next to the wire baskets on the third shelf in the storeroom. I thought I might display them next to the counter on that piece of burgundy velvet. What do you think?"

"Sounds awesome, Paula. I never would have thought of that. Was I smart, or was I smart to hire you?" I gave her an affectionate pat on the shoulder.

"Kiddo, what do you mean, *hire* me? Andy and I chose *you*. Once we decided we wanted to work here, you never had a chance." She winked at me and turned back to her work.

I piddled around in the storeroom for awhile and then headed to Angles, anxious to get Janie alone and pump her for information about Charley. No such luck.

19

As soon as I walked in the door I saw Emile, the owner and sole stylist. The name "Emile" conjures up an image of a suave, debonair, French lover. The reality is quite different. Emile Schwartz is short, fat, and balding, and browbeats his clients. He wears a permanent sneer, and the only reason he has so many clients is because he is a genius at styling hair.

"You need a hair cut. You look like shit," he greeted me.

"Hello, Emile. How nice to see you," I replied through gritted teeth. "Maybe you can fit me in tomorrow?"

"Talk to Janie. Goin' to be busy because of the big dance on Saturday. Can't promise you anything." And off he went.

Janie's manicure station is to the right of the reception desk, positioned so that she can look out the window at the passersby in case she has a boring client. I glanced over at her, and she gave me a sympathetic look. Janie also works as the receptionist.

"Let me look at the schedule, Penny. I might be able to squeeze you in during lunch. Emile is only here until three o'clock tomorrow." We settled on a twelve-thirty appointment for tomorrow, Friday. That way my nails and hair would look good for the dance.

I have a weekly appointment with Janie to shape and buff my nails. She refuses to put polish on them because, she says, "It would be like putting sauce on the turkey." I don't understand that, but I respect her professional opinion.

"Penny, how is the book coming along?" Janie and I have been talking about THE BOOK for a long time now. We have been bouncing some ideas around, and she has given me lots of suggestions regarding who to kill and how to kill them. She has the face of an angel and a diabolical twist of mind. Janie must be all of twenty-two-years old, and has the fresh, clean look of a girl scout, even though her naturally blond hair is often purple or orange, and she can wear ten earrings at a time without her ears drooping. Mom must have told her that I was getting close to starting my murder mystery.

"Well, I have the first few paragraphs written."

Janie clapped her pinked-tipped hands until I got dizzy. "Oh, goody. Can I be in it? Who is going to die? Is it Amelia Borden?"

Amelia Borden is a sixty-year-old widow who lives directly across the street from me on Fifth Street, in a Gothic Revival-style house. She writes horror stories, and her house is reputedly haunted. Amelia is somewhat of a recluse, and the fact that she has a hunky young but-ler/chauffeur named Tony has sparked much interest and conversation around the neighborhood. Amelia is Janie's least favorite client because she doesn't tip.

I gave a noncommittal answer to the effect that I ha-ven't thought that far ahead yet and tried to steer the conversation to the topic of Charley Walker. Janie was still in a training bra during the "Lannie and Charley era," but she is privy to all sorts of information. I hesi-tated a moment and asked, "Did I see Stella leave a few minutes ago? Mom said that she saw her getting her hair done yesterday. Didn't she like the cut?"

"Yeah, she was in, but it wasn't about her hair. I had to fix a broken nail." Silence. This wasn't going to be easy.

21

"Uh, Mom said something about a conversation about somebody named Charley," I prodded.

Janie puckered her brow and thought for a moment. "I don't know about that. I do know that Stella seemed all excited today about a big date for the dance. She said that she was going to 'turn a few heads around here.' I really didn't understand what she was talking about. You know how Stella can be."

Yeah, I knew how Stella could be, and it worried me.

"Hey, Penny, how about Amelia being electrocuted under the dryer?"… file, file, buff, buff…"Or, she can be scalded to death getting her hair washed…."

I finally made my escape. I looked across the street as I left the salon and was tempted to make a neighborly visit to the owner of the soon-to-be-open Full of Beans. Would I look too forward? I looked at my watch and figured that I should give our relationship a little time. It had only been two hours and forty-five minutes since I bade farewell to Derek. I know. I'll stop in tomorrow and bring him some homemade breakfast rolls on my way to work. I smiled. I had a plan.

***

Lannie's favorite wine is Lambert Bridge merlot, so I took a two-block detour on the way home to Hausfrau Haven to pick up a bottle. I was thinking that a glass or two might help soften the news about Charley. Hmm… maybe I should get two bottles. I was in the kitchen cooking when I heard the click of the dead bolt. I glanced at the clock and figured that

Thomas and Taylor were here. Those two can smell food a mile away.

"Hola, Penny. Mamá nos dijo que cenáramos aquí." Thomas walked into the kitchen, followed by Taylor. He snagged an apple from the fruit bowl and gave me a big smile.

"Et tu, Brute?" I smiled back.

"Mom told us to speak Spanish this summer to help her practice." The twins have been taking Spanish since the third grade and are fluent. I am the only one in the family without the language gene. I have visions of myself at family gatherings, sitting alone in the kitchen, while everyone else is in the family room laughing and talking in Spanish. Maybe I should look into some Adult Ed classes.

"Tell me about your first day of summer vacation. Are you bored yet?"

"No way, Penny. We went over to Whimsies and helped Andy unpack some boxes. Can we work weekends for you? We need the money."

I looked over at them while I considered a reply. They really are great kids. P.J. and I were thirteen when they were born, and they were like our pets. They were the cutest little babies. Now they are tall and slender like our father was, with Mom's good, blond looks. P.J. and I have the same lanky build, but with Dad's dark hair and brown eyes. Taylor and Thomas were only six-years old when Dad died, and Mom, P.J., and I have tried to keep his memory alive for them. They are well-adjusted, normal teenagers, and I credit Mom for doing an exemplary job raising them.

"Let me talk to Alice, but I think it should be okay. Why do you need the money?"

"We entered a contest at school. It's a summer project; the winner will be announced right after school starts in the fall. All we have to do is submit a video tape of a documentary…"

"We get to pick out the topic," Taylor piped in.

"…and the winner's tape will be aired on public television. That's why we need the money — to buy a video camera."

"It will take you half the summer to earn enough to buy a video camera, because I can only use you on weekends."

Taylor beamed at me. "But we have another job, too. We start on Tuesday. We filled out a job application this afternoon and were hired on the spot."

"No kidding. That's great! Where are you working?"

"Full of Beans. Mr. D'Amico runs the place, and he said we could call him Derek. He's really cool. He asked us if you were our sister, and when we said 'yes,' he said that was good enough for him. How do you know him?"

"Mom and I met him this morning at Schiller Park. I spent a total of five minutes with him, but I guess I made an impression. Um, did he say anything else about me?"

"No. What are we having for dinner? Are you making a spaghetti casserole?"

"Uh huh." Darn! I was hoping Derek poured his heart out to them. "Taylor, could you please cube some cheddar cheese for me, and Thomas, how about getting the salad ready? Lannie is coming over so throw in another tomato." I always have trouble getting all the food ready at one time when I'm cooking several different dishes. P.J. suggested making casseroles whenever possible. I always serve casseroles now whenever I have company, and I love the "no worry" cooking method.

Casserole in the oven, wine uncorked, we were good to go. Our other guest was expected at any moment. Thomas went off to the den to play on the computer while we waited, and Taylor sat down at the counter and watched me clean up.

"Penny, do you think you could help me with my makeup this Saturday? Ben Doyle is coming to the dance, and I want to look extra special."

"Is that your friend Zoë's brother?"

"Yeah. Zoë said he thinks I'm cute. He's a year ahead of us at school, and I never even thought he knew I was alive. Can you help me out?"

"Sure, honey, you'll blow him away. Come over in the afternoon, and I'll see what I can do." It was a bittersweet moment. I didn't want my baby sister to grow up, but, on the other hand, I was proud of the young woman she was becoming. This Ben just better not break her heart, or he'd have the entire Mitchell clan to deal with.

Tatters started barking, announcing Lannie's arrival. She came back to the kitchen carrying a big white box. "I see Flossie and Freddy are here." Lannie loves to make allusions to the Bobbsey twins.

Thomas was close on her heels, and asked, "Are those cream puffs from Schmidt's Sausage Haus?" He was practically drooling.

"Uh huh. I stopped on my way over because we are celebrating tonight. I am a free woman for the next three months, and I'm a party waiting to happen. Who wants to join me?"

Of course, we were all game to help Lannie celebrate. It wouldn't be right to let her party alone.

"Have you started the book, Penelope?" She pro-
nounced my name to rhyme with "cantaloupe." That has
been her pet name for me since we were kids.

"I can honestly say that the book is twice as long this
afternoon as it was this morning."

Lannie spied the wine on the counter, poured herself
a glass, and raised it to me, saying, "Here's to the next
P.D. James."

We carried the food into the dining room and sat
down to a delicious meal, if I do say so myself. Taylor
and Thomas were full of enthusiasm about their video
project, and Lannie was interested in hearing all the details.

"Have you kids thought of a topic?"

Taylor answered since Thomas was busy stuffing
bread into his mouth. "We thought we might do a
documentary about laundromat people."

Lannie and I smiled at each other over the rims of
our wine glasses. She is a "laundromat person," and I
was one up until six months ago, when I bought my
handy-dandy stackable washer and dryer.

"What approach are you going to take?"

"We want to show that laundromat users represent a
microcosm of the best that society has to offer. They are
generous, except with their laundry soap, and they are
very considerate of other people's space. We want to
interview them and film them in action."

The part about the laundry soap is true. I always sat
with my detergent on my lap for fear that someone
would snatch it from me.

Lannie was surprised and delighted. "That's an original approach, and I think you might just have something there. I always feel very vulnerable when I'm doing a load of underwear, and appreciate the discretion of the other patrons."

Over dessert we moved on to the topic of the talent show. The twins asked Lannie to play the piano to provide some background music to help make their magic act more dramatic.

"Sure, I'd be happy to. But I'm surprised your mom is going to let you do another magic act."

"Mom said we could, as long as we didn't use any live animals this year."

Lannie and I took a moment to relish the memory of last year's fiasco. One of the pigeons escaped from its cage during the show and flew into the audience. It fell in love with Stella Morgan's hat and decided to perch there. She screamed and jumped up and down, trying to dislodge it. The poor pigeon was so upset that it pooped all over Stella's hat. She was a sight with pigeon poop dripping from her hat onto her Evan Picone jacket.

My capacity for Christian charity is stretched to the limit when it comes to Stella. It is even worse for Lannie. There were rumors at the time of her breakup with Charley that he was having an affair. It could never be confirmed, but Lannie and I suspected that Stella — the trois part of the ménage, the obtuse section of the love triangle — was offering Charley her services, and I don't mean as a realtor. Charley often came to the Brewery District (adjacent to German Village) to drink and carouse with his friends. We assumed that he met Stella during one of his forays.

"Hey, kids, I'll make a deal with you. Lannie and I will clean up if you take Tatters for a walk." The deal was sealed, and I poured Lannie and myself another glass of wine to make cleanup more fun.

I said a little prayer for inspiration and took the plunge. "Lannie, Charley Walker is back in town." How's that for slipping the news into the conversation? I could have kicked myself when I saw her face go pale and her knees buckle. "Are you okay? Sit down; I'll get you some water."

"Whew. I'm okay, thanks. Just a little surprised is all. I thought that part of my life was over, and now he's back" —she snapped her fingers — "just like that. Just give me a minute to get used to the idea."

No one knows what happened to Charley since the divorce. His mother moved to Colorado to be close to her sister, and Charley just disappeared. One of his friends at the time said he had moved to Dayton. We never questioned his leaving; we were just thankful for our good luck.

"How do you know he's back? Have you seen him?"

"No. Mom heard about it at 'Tangles'" — I used our little joke in hopes of eliciting a smile — "but the details are sketchy. I had my nails done this afternoon and asked Janie, but she didn't know anything. I'm getting my hair cut tomorrow, so I'll see if Emile can tell me anything. Come on, let's take our wine out to the front porch swing and watch the tourists go by. That will cheer you up."

Lannie and I have spent many a lazy night on that swing, enjoying the oohs and ahs of the Village visitors as they walk up and down the street. There is a great deal to attract attention: the window boxes overflowing with vividly-colored flowers, the hitching posts and carriage stoops lining the streets at intervals, bringing to mind the bygone days of our great-grandparents, attractive mailboxes wrought of iron in every shape imaginable, and the well-tended gardens. I am extremely pleased to be part of this fascinating neighborhood.

Tatters and the kids were just coming in the front gate as we got settled on the swing. Tatters is always happy to see me, even after a ten-minute absence. His tail wags enthusiastically, and he dances up and down. It's nice to be loved.

"Did you have a good walk?"

Tatters gave me a "woof, woof," which means "yes." Out of the corner of my eye, I saw Mom's fire-engine red Volvo round the corner.

"Good timing, Taylor and Thomas. Mom's here."

My mother pulled up to the curb in front of the house and got out. "Hola. Estoy de vuelta."

"How did the performance go?"

"Muy bien. The mall manager asked the choir to come back for a repeat performance. John, the choir director, told me he thinks I'm improving." She puffed up with pride. Lannie and I avoided eye contact. If there were a soprano version of Louis Armstrong, Mom would be it.

"Why did you drive over, Mom?"

"I thought the kids and I would go over to see Lily before she gets settled in for the night. It might be dark by the time we get home. I haven't seen my granddaughter for two whole days. What do you think, kids? Do you want to go over for a little visit?"

"Sure."

"Yeah."

"Taylor has my shawl, Mom. Enjoy it." As the twins got into the car, Mom stood at her car door, looking from Lannie to me, and raised her eyebrows. I gave a slight nod.

"Lannie, if you need me for anything, I want you to call. Remember, Saint Theresa says that we are all right where we are supposed to be, so this is happening for a reason."

Lannie smiled at my mother with true affection. "Angela, I'm going to be just fine. Don't worry about anything, honest."

We sat in silence and watched the Volvo's taillights disappear down the street. After a bit, Lannie squeezed my hand and said, "I am going to be fine. They are both right, your mother and Saint Theresa, that is. Charley's return has nothing to do with me. He can't hurt me anymore unless I let him, and I've come too far to let that happen. I'm right where I am supposed to be, doing exactly what I'm supposed to be doing. Let's finish off the wine."

Chapter 3

He laughed out loud at the raging storm. One can't just observe a storm; one has to participate in it, willingly or not. He scoffed at those who cower from the awesome fury of the gods. He embraced the danger, the excitement. He had won. Two more souls now belonged to him...

Okay, now what? I've heard of this happening — the dreaded writer's block. I should have expected it; after all, I had written nearly sixty words. Stay calm and don't think about it. Step away from the computer and pretend everything is normal. I was a fool to start writing so early this morning, especially after the late night and the wine. Never again, I vowed.

I should have known better. What little sleep I did get last night was interrupted by Tatters's snoring. He insists on sleeping next to me and hogs most of the bed. I woke up at six to those damn chirping birds and couldn't get back to sleep. I don't usually go to the shop until nine, so I thought I'd use my time wisely to work on the book. We got up early, and I followed Tatters down the steps and through the kitchen to the back door. Was Tatters staggering, or were my eyes wobbling? I turned on the coffee pot, wove my way to the bathroom, and made the mistake of looking in the mirror. How did my hair know I had too much to drink? Oh well—I remembered my appointment at Angles and decided to go with the wild-woman look until then. Then I thought about going to Derek's shop before work, and plugged in the curling iron for a quick fix. The burn on my forehead is a testament to that bad decision. I taped a used teabag to my forehead (Mom swears it takes the redness out) and thought it would be safer for me to sit and write than to wander around the house.

So, here I am, more depressed than ever. What happened to that sweet, cheerful Penny Mitchell who used to live in my body? I was getting into a pretty deep funk when the doorbell chimed.

"Penny darling, it's Mom. Are you up?"

I could see the silhouette of her little head through the leaded glass. I unlocked the door and said, "This is not a good time, Mom. What are you doing here at" — I glanced at my watch — "seven o'clock in the morning? And what is in the Tupperware?"

She glanced sympathetically at my forehead and patted me on the shoulder. "As for this" — she tapped the container with her index finger — "es una sorpresa," she chirped, and skipped toward the kitchen. "I made some sticky buns and thought you might like a few."

How does my mother know just what I need? It scares me sometimes. When we were little she would tell P.J. and me that she had "mommy radar." We believed it then, and I believe it now.

"I would love a sticky bun. The coffee is ready. Want to have some with me?"

"No, gracias. Taylor and Thomas are still sleeping, and I want to get home before they wake up. I really just wanted to know how Lannie took the news about Charley and if she is going to be all right."

"She was shocked at first, but she convinced me that she is okay with this. I'm not sure what will happen if she runs into him, but it doesn't seem to bother her that they share the same zip code. I'm meeting her for lunch after I get my hair cut, and we'll see how things are after she's had a night to sleep on it."

"Good. Call me if you need me and have a muy buen día."

I walked her to the door. "Adiós, Mom, and thanks for the buns."

"De nada. Hasta la vista."

My day had taken a turn for the better. Now I had some sticky buns to drop off to Derek on my way to work. Tatters and I went upstairs to get dressed. Well, Tatters watched while I got dressed. Sometimes I take him to the shop with me if I'm going to be working in the office, or if Paula and Andy are both there. That way I can take him out for a potty break if he needs one, without leaving the shop unattended. Today, he was going to be sad because I was leaving the shop for an extended period to get my hair done and have lunch with Lannie. He would just have to tough it out at home.

My walk to work is less than three blocks, and today was one of those days when I could stretch it into a ten-minute stroll. The sun was filtering through trees, creating flattering shadows on the houses and streets. I call this the "dappler effect." The delivery trucks were starting their rounds to the various establishments in the Village. Several people were out and about, some walking with purpose, and some just enjoying the morning. I passed my neighbor, Amelia Borden, as we each turned the corner on Kossuth at the same time, heading in different directions.

"Good morning, Ms. Borden. I see you've been out shopping already." I nodded toward the bakery sack in her hand.

"Good morning, dear. Yes, I had a craving for some cinnamon rolls from Juergen's Bakery." Amelia Borden is an aging beauty who could have been a famous film star in the 1950s or 1960s. She writes bestsellers in the horror genre. Not my taste but, hey, somebody has to do it. I was too embarrassed to tell her about my new book for fear that she would want to read it and not like it. At this point in my career as an author, I don't think I can handle the criticism. "It's Tony's day off and I like to get out on my own. I feel I should use his services when he is at home."

Tony Delamar is Amelia's butler and driver. He is not the typical stiff English butler; he is muscular and good looking in a smarmy sort of way. His "uniform" is dark slacks and a white shirt. Tony lives in the carriage house at the rear of Amelia's property, and I rarely see him. He has worked for her for at least the three years I have been living across from her. I see him from time to time when I'm working in my front garden. He doesn't ever speak to me; he just stands staring at me while I do my work. Tony gives me the creeps.

"Well, nice seeing you, Ms. Borden. I'm due at the shop now. Enjoy your rolls."

"I will, dear. Have a pleasant day." It never ceases to amaze me that her lovely face hides a twisted mind.

A few minutes later, I arrived at Full of Beans. I glanced across the street to my store and saw my partner, Alice, through the window. I held up a finger to indicate that I would be there in a minute. She nodded and waved. I took a deep breath, gave a perfunctory knock on the door, and let myself in.

Wow, this was great! There were several round tables with ice cream parlor-type chairs positioned at the front of the shop and a tall wooden counter, flanked by bakery cases, at the rear. Shelves filled with bags of coffee and coffee-drinking accoutrements lined the walls. The red-and-white-checked café curtains on the windows gave the shop a nostalgic, comfortable feeling. I looked around for Derek and was disappointed when Max came through the doorway at the rear of the shop.

Max is the scruffy, grumpy Village handyman of indeterminate age, anywhere from forty to one-hundred forty, who does jobs for me and the other residents and shop owners. I always keep a supply of bandages on hand whenever he does work for me because that man is one walking scar. He must have learned his trade by trial and error, but he does good work and he's cheap.

"Hello, Max."

"Humph."

Ah, chatty as ever. "Is Derek around?"

"Nope."

"Uh, do you know when he'll be back?"

"Nope."

"I'm going to leave this box on the counter with a little note. Will you make sure to tell him I was here?"

"Yep."

"Thanks, Max. I'll be seeing you around."

"S'long."

Alice gave me a wry little smile when I entered Whimsies. "I didn't know you had a 'thing' for Max."

"I'm just playing Cupid for you, Alice. You two were made for each other." We both giggled at that. Thankfully, she didn't ask me why I was at the new store, but I suspected she had a good idea. Alice and I got busy inventorying some new merchandise while Paula and Andy took care of the customers. I spent a few hours on the books and was ready for a break by the time I had to leave for my appointment.

"I'm leaving now, but I should be back at around two, if that's okay with everybody. I'm having a quick lunch with Lannie after my hair appointment, and then I'm stopping at home to check on Tatters. I'll probably bring him back with me."

"That's fine," they all answered in unison.

Andy added, "Thanks, Penny, for staying late so Paula and I can go to the movies. We haven't had a night out in a while and this is a real treat."

"No problem. Happy to do it."

A short walk of fifty feet had me at Angles, ready to face Emile and a half hour of his surly self.

"Hi, Janie," I greeted as I walked in. "I'll just sit here with you until Emile is ready for me."

"Hiya, Penny, how…"

"Come back, I'm waiting."

"I guess he's ready. See you soon."

I walked through the reception area into the salon and sat at the third and last seat from the window. Emile is the only stylist in the salon, so I don't understand why there are three stations. He looked at me and shook his head, pointing to window seat. I hate it when anyone who walks by can see me through the glass. It's demeaning to be stared at while getting beautified. I meekly moved to the first chair.

"Sit down, uncross your legs, and take your earrings out." Emile sure has a way with words. My hair always looks good when I leave, but my ego is bruised and battered.

"Whadda ya want to do with your hair today?"

"Well, I saw this neat way of cutting hair on TV. You take a section and twist it, then cut it. The end result is a style that is fluffy and resistant to wind and rain. I'd like to try it." I looked at him hopefully.

"Hmm. Don't know that one, but there's always a first time. Let me think a minute." He walked around my chair, considering me from all angles, picked up his scissors, gave a few practice clicks, and started in on the creative process.

Thirty minutes later he turned off the blow dryer and stood back to admire his work. I was pleased with the results. I looked like a fluffy-headed Audrey Hepburn.

"Thanks, Emile, I really like the cut. You did a nice job."

"You have nice hair."

I couldn't believe the compliment. I have been coming here for more than five years, and this is the very first time Emile has said something nice to me. I must really look good.

I heard voices from the reception area and figured that Lannie had arrived for our lunch date. I thanked Emile and went out to pay Janie. Then, I remembered that I had forgotten to ask Emile about Charley, what with all the trauma about sitting in the window seat. I couldn't do it now, so I thought I'd try to catch him later in the day.

Lannie was standing just inside the door with her hands balled into fists behind her back, chatting away with Janie. I understood perfectly. Lannie maintains that teachers have summer vacations so that their hands can heal. She says they should receive hazard pay for the paper cuts, permanently ink-stained palms, and chalk-encrusted cuticles. Her hands are not fit for viewing until at least the end of July, and she was shielding Janie from their deplorable state.

"You look terrific, Penelope."

Janie was looking perplexed. "Why does Lannie say your name that way?"

"What way?"

"You know, to rhyme with 'envelope'?'"

"Oh, it's just a pet name she has for me."

"Why would she give you a pet's name?"

Lannie and I looked at each other helplessly and shrugged. Sometimes I wonder if the number of Janie's brain cells even reaches double digits.

Lannie spoke again. "I really do like your hair. I wonder if I could get mine to do that."

"No," Emile barked from the salon area.

We all smiled at each other, and Lannie and I left on that note.

"You realize that Emile hasn't liked me ever since I asked him to tint my hair. He said it was a sacrilege to mess with 'that glorious shade of copper,' so he punished me by making me look like Marge Simpson."

I remembered that hairdo. She really did look kind of funny. Lannie stands five-ten in her stocking feet, and really didn't need the extra fourteen inches.

"Do you want to grab a sandwich from the Brown Bag Deli and take it to the park?" I asked.

"Sounds like a plan to me."

A few minutes later, we were seated at a picnic table in Schiller Park, enjoying the sunshine and watching the squirrels chase each other. Lannie assured me that she was fine after our discussion last night, and I believed her.

"Penny, I took a vow in front of God and two hundred people to be good to Charley. I always have and I always will honor that vow, even if I am not with him. He was bad for me and brought out the very worst in me, but I pray for him and wish him the best, even though he was a dastard…"

"A dastard?"

"Angela told me I had to clean up my language, so I'm getting creative — yes, a dastard. But I have forgiven him and am just grateful that he is out of my life. End of discussion."

I stood up, gathered up the garbage, and gave her a little pat on the shoulder.

"You're awesome, Lannie, I don't care what anyone else says. Come on, I'll walk you part of the way home. I have to get Tatters because Paula and Andy are leaving early to catch the new Harrison Ford film, and I'm working late."

We reached my house and could see Tatters in the window. He loves to sit on the back of the couch and look out the window, watching everybody's business. Lannie and I said "good-bye," and I unlocked the door and hugged Tatters.

"Hi, baby, I got groomed today. Do I look beautiful? Do you want to go to work now, you lazy beast?"

Tatters and I got to the shop and settled in the office to do some paperwork. Alice was busy with some customers, but came back to see me later to hand me a note.

"This was delivered for you."

I took the note, opened it and read —

"I enjoyed the sticky buns. That was very nice of you to bring me breakfast. Penny, there is no need to thank me for hiring Taylor and Thomas. If they are anything like their mom and big sister, I got a bargain. I look forward to the dance tomorrow night. Maybe you can save a dance or two for me. D."

Oh, how sweet! I reread the note and noticed Alice still standing there, regarding me with a bemused smile.

"What?" I said. "It's just a little thank-you note."

"If you say so." She turned and walked back to the customer area. Alice and Mom are two of a kind. I can't have any private feelings without them knowing about it. My mom met Alice years ago when Dad was sick, and they became close friends. Alice owned and operated a hospice care center. She hired and trained professional medical personnel to care for the sick. Alice doesn't like to talk about the old days. She burned out after twenty years of health care work and decided to buy a little business here in the Village. I came to work for her after I graduated from college and, over the years, have gained her trust and confidence. Three years ago she offered to make me her partner. Just recently, she has started making noises about retiring; I'm not sure how I feel about that.

At three o'clock, I decided to catch Emile before he left for the day. I remembered that Janie had told me that was when the shop was closing for the day. I left through the front door and told Alice I would be back soon and to please keep an eye on Tatters. I walked three doors down and tried the front door, but it was locked. I peered through the front window and didn't see anyone. Then I thought I would go around to the alley and see if Emile might be in his office in the back of the salon. As I approached the delivery door, I could hear voices. The door was ajar, so I stood next to it, out of sight, so as not to interrupt Emile and his visitor. I didn't mean to eavesdrop, not really. I just wanted to figure out how long I had to wait. I would have gone in had one of the voices belonged to Janie. It didn't. Every newly-shaved hair on the back of my neck stood on end as I listened with alarm.

"Well, that's just too damn bad, isn't it? I don't care about any of that now. I stayed away for seven long years, and now I'm back, and I can do anything I please."

That voice belonged to Charley, and it was making my skin crawl. I had forgotten about the effect he could have on me. Memory is a funny thing. We mold it and shape it and distort it until it becomes something we can live with. Lannie might be wishing him well, but I was just wishing him away.

I heard Emile answer, "Just leave her alone and get outta here. You make me sick."

I ran on tippy toes to the corner of the alley and hoped that, when he left, Charley would turn right and not see me. I turned the corner and flattened myself against the brick wall of the building. I heard the door slam and footsteps walk in the other direction. I breathed a sigh of relief. No way was I going back to Angles to innocently ask Emile about Charley. I would go back to Whimsies, finish out the day, and then do a lot of thinking. I remembered what Grandma Mitchell always said: "When things start out bad, they tend to stay bad." I hoped that wouldn't be the case.

Chapter 4

Kevin woke up slowly, aware only of a splitting headache. He tried to shift to make himself more comfortable, but was unable to move. He opened his eyes to total blackness. "Where am I? What is going on?" he thought. "Miranda?" He heard an answering whimper. "Miranda, what the hell is happening?"

One game of Snood and I'll get back to the story. I promise, just one more game. When I turned twenty-five I figured it was time to give up my video games, so I donated my beloved Tetras and Dr. Mario to Taylor and Thomas. I really missed playing, so I downloaded Snood on to my computer to get my daily fix. There is nothing like shooting a row of little critters and having them disappear. It makes me feel powerful and in control of my life. I may be delusional, but I'm happy. I rationalized that I had worked enough for today, and turned my thoughts to the dance tonight. Getting ready for a special event is always fun. There is an excitement and anticipation in the air that is as pleasurable as the event, sometimes even more so. Tatters was excited, and he wasn't even going to the dance.

I took extra pains to look nice when it was time to get dressed. I was pleased with my new haircut and the simple, knee-length lavender sheath with the six inch slit up each side. The lavender color tends to bring out the rose tones in my olive complexion. With my strappy,

high-heeled sandals and my dangly rhinestone earrings I was a man killer. Derek D'Amico, you won't
stand a chance!

I got to Legion Hall a little bit early to help P.J. and
Grace set up their hors d'oeuvres. Other people had signed
up to bring food, so they didn't have to do everything, but
their food is always the first to go. P.J. and Grace are a
handsome couple, he with his tall build and dark coloring
and Grace with her petite build and strawberry-blond hair.
They set me to work placing scallops rumaki, chicken sa-
tay, Swedish meatballs, clams casino, and petit fours on
the buffet table next to the punch bowl.

By the time we finished setting up the food, the
dance hall was filling with people. I saw Lannie coming
toward us and took a moment to admire how pretty she
looked in a black sundress sprinkled with tiny, yellow
flowers.

"Hullo, dahling, I'm sooo glad you could come," I
trilled.

P.J. gave an admiring wolf whistle and Grace gave
him a mock punch on the shoulder.

"If you don't leave my poor, misguided husband
alone, Lannie, I'm going to take you outside and have
my mother-in-law beat you up."

Lannie laughed. "Now that would scare me. He's all
yours, Grace. Besides, I know way too much about him
to ever be bowled over by his handsome face."

Lannie and I stood by the buffet trying to decide
where to start. She glanced over my shoulder and said,
"Don't look now. Here comes 'Hell on Heels'." I turned
and saw Stella clickety-clicking toward us with a tray
filled with food.

Stella blew air kisses toward us. "Penny, Lannie, how are you?" She gave us the once-over and turned toward Lannie. "I guess it's a myth."

I took the bait. "What's a myth, Stella?"

"That black can be slimming. Lannie, maybe you shouldn't be standing by the food. You know how hard it is to lose those pesky extra pounds."

That was unfair. Lannie's dress showed off her voluptuous figure, and she really did look beautiful; next to her, Stella looked like a scarecrow. I quickly intervened before Lannie could skewer her with that sharp tongue of hers. "Hey, Stella, what do you have there? Sure looks good."

"Oh, I made my world-famous shrimp balls."

Lannie quipped, "I didn't know shrimp had b...umph." I hurriedly stuffed an olive in Lannie's mouth. Lannie swallowed the olive, and I saw an unholy gleam in her eye. "Say, Stella, how would you like to join us tomorrow morning for a friendly game of volleyball? You look like an athlete to me."

Lannie and I play jungle-rules volleyball at the recreation center every Sunday morning at eleven o'clock, right after Mass, and I wouldn't call the games exactly "friendly." I am the shortest one on the team at five-eight, and my teammates call me "munchkin." Stella stands at five-eight in her stiletto heels, and I don't think those are allowed on the court. I glanced at her hands and noted her two-inch long nails. No, as annoying as she is, I couldn't let Stella be goaded into playing. My conscience kicked in and I started to say, "Stella ..."

She interrupted me. "Yes, I am athletic. I was a middle school pom-pom girl." I heard Lannie snort. "By the way, Penny, where is the elf?"

45

The gloves were off. I knew she was referring to my mother, who is really only half elf. "Mom will be here soon. See you at ten forty-five at the rec center, Stella."

Lannie and I wandered off in different directions to visit and mingle with the other party-goers. The band was setting up to play. It was the same band as last year, and everyone enjoys their music. They play a variety of songs to please all age groups. I was chatting with some friends I hadn't seen for a while when I happened to glance to the back of the hall where the restrooms and coat racks are situated. That part of the hall was more dimly lit than the dance area, but I could make out at least one familiar figure in conversation with someone. I excused myself from my friends and nonchalantly headed toward the restroom area. I spied a potted palm about five feet away from the two people and, checking over my shoulder to be sure no one was watching, stepped behind it.

Charley was talking animatedly to Tony Delamar, Amelia Borden's butler. It had been years since I had seen Charley, but some people have a unique way of carrying themselves that make them easily recognizable, even after years of absence. Charley was still handsome in a dissipated sort of way. He was just thirty, but the wiry, athletic build was long gone. He was about twenty-five pounds heavier now, with pouches under his eyes and a beer belly. Luckily, they were so engrossed in their conversation that they didn't notice me behind the plant. I couldn't make out exactly what they were saying because they were speaking in low voices, but I could detect a sense of urgency in their exchange.

"What do you mean…? I didn't…"

"Keep…to…secret."

They walked back toward the dance floor, and I stayed put for a bit. I felt frustrated not being able to figure out why they were even talking, and was deep in thought. A hand touched my shoulder and I jumped. I turned and saw Mr. Green Eyes smiling at me.

"So it *is* you," he said. "I was curious about the potted palm wearing high heels. You're not shy are you?" He gave me a bemused smile, then stepped back to take in my outfit. "You look absolutely gorgeous."

As happy as I was to see him, I was just as embarrassed to be caught spying. "Uh, thanks, Derek, you look gorgeous yourself." And he did. He was wearing dark slacks and a camel blazer over a lavender shirt with a coordinating tie. "We both had the same idea…Wearing lavender, I mean." Lord, give me inspiration. "I was just standing here thinking… Do you want something to drink?"

"That would be good. You know, I always think better myself when I have the chance to talk things over with a plant." He made me feel at ease with the lopsided grin he sent my way. "Do you want something from the bar or just the punch?"

I remembered my last encounter with "the grape," and wasn't quite ready to try it again. "The punch will be fine, thanks. But you get whatever you want."

We walked back toward the center of the hall, and Derek went off to get our drinks. I saw Mom and the kids making their way toward me and sent them a little wave. Mom looked pretty in a simple blue sundress that matched her eyes, and my shawl looked good slung over her arm. The twins looked so grown up. Thomas was wearing a navy sport coat with gray slacks, and Taylor looked beautiful in a tea-length yellow dress.

"You guys are a walking advertisement for the superiority of the Mitchell gene pool."

"Buenas noches, Penny, y gracias."

I took my drink from Derek as he joined our little group. I whispered an aside to Taylor. "I saw the object of your affections standing with that group of kids over by the entrance." The twins said their "hellos" to Derek and took off toward their group of friends.

"Thanks for the drink, Derek."

"You're welcome." He turned toward my mother. "Angela, estás muy bonita esta noche. El color del vestido es el mismo que los ojos. Y los hijos son terríficos."

Mom beamed at him, and I said, "I didn't know you could speak Spanish."

"I took a few years in college, and I confess to brushing up a bit before the dance to impress your mother."

"Well, I'm duly impressed," said Mom. "It's good to see you again, Derek, and thanks for the compliment. By the way, do you have any talents?" I shot her a warning glance. She ignored me and continued. "You see, there is a talent show coming up next week, and I was wondering if you'd be interested in performing."

"I used to play the sax, but that was years ago. I don't think I would be a good choice, Angela."

"Just think about it, okay? I'll see you two later. I'm going to grab some of P.J.'s hors d'oeuvres before they disappear."

"Derek," I warned, "my mother is relentless. She bats those baby blues and it's hard to say 'no.' I've had years of practice; you're just a novice. Repeat after me, n-o, no."

"Don't worry, Penny. If she heard me play she would change her mind. Would you like to dance? I brushed up on my dance steps, although I'll admit that Loretta isn't the best partner. I only hope nobody was peeking through the window when we did our dips and twirls."

I was flattered and, of course, said "yes." The band was playing "Unchained Melody," my all-time favorite romantic song. We put our drinks on the nearest table, and he took me in his arms and swept me away to the center of the dance floor. We fit together just right. I was grateful for the sea of bodies, which gave us an excuse to move even closer together. Even though I was wearing high heels, he was tall enough that I could nestle my left cheek between his neck and right shoulder. I gave a sigh of contentment, and could feel his smile as his chin rested on the top of my head. I was having wonderful thoughts as the music ended. Life was good. The other couples began to drift off the dance floor, and I started to lift my head to thank Derek and give him my biggest smile, but I was stuck. Somehow my earring had caught on the fabric of his jacket, and I couldn't move my head, not even an inch.

"Derek," I frantically whispered, "my earring is caught on your jacket and I can't move my head."

"Let me see if I can help." I felt his right hand fiddling around trying to extricate my uncooperative earring from his jacket. "I can't seem to find the problem. Maybe if I take off my…"

"Ow, you're pulling my ear off."

"Sorry. Just hold on a minute. I'm sure the band is getting ready to start another song, and we'll have some time to think about this."

By now we were totally alone on the dance floor, my head stuck on his shoulder, unable to move, and attracting the attention of those nearby. At that moment the band started with a lively rendition of "The Beer Barrel Polka."

Oh, God, help me! "I can't do the Polka."

"Neither can I. Listen, Penny, here's the plan. We are going to dance nonchalantly through the crowd toward that open doorway to the patio. Once we're there, we can figure out what to do."

"But I can't see where I'm going. Remember, all I can see is your Adam's apple."

"That's okay. I can see to navigate. Just follow me."

"I have no choice." I felt his shoulder twitch. "You had better not be laughing." I found absolutely no humor in the situation.

"No, no. Um, I'm just stifling a sneeze."

We started to move slowly among the whirling Polka dancers. I couldn't see much, but every once in a while I caught a glimpse of a surprised or amused face as we made our exit.

Finally! Once on the patio, Derek made short work of freeing my earring. "You know, Penny, I'm always going to think of 'The Beer Barrel Polka' as our song." He smiled and chucked me on the chin.

"You do think this is funny, don't you? Well, give me another fifty years and I might think so too." I looked at him, saw his lips start to twitch, and couldn't help myself. We both started to laugh and couldn't stop.

Murder, *Murder*

"I didn't realize that you were going to be the entertainment for tonight. Your mom is probably going to want that act for the talent show." I turned and saw that Lannie had come out to the patio.

I took a deep breath to quell the laughter; I was in danger of wetting my pants. "Lannie, I want you to meet Derek D'Amico. He's brand new in town and is the owner of Full of Beans. Derek, this is my best friend, Lannie Daugherty."

"A pleasure."

"Nice to meet you."

Lannie sent me a questioning look that I understood perfectly.

"Derek and I met at the park the other day. Actually, my dog picked up his dog. Tatters has a thing for Loretta."

"Loretta?"

"You'll understand once you see her."

I could tell that something was a little "off" with Lannie. Normally, a situation such as this would have had her rolling on the floor. She was being polite and charming, and no one else would have noticed anything amiss.

I looked at Derek and said, "Will you excuse us for a little bit while we go freshen up? You know that girls can't go to the powder room by themselves."

"Please go, Penny. I saw some people from the Shop Owners' Association, and I want to talk to them. Let me know when you are ready for another dance." He winked at me and stopped my heart.

"See you in a bit, Derek."

Lannie and I made our way to the restroom. I opened the door and peeked in to make sure it was empty, then motioned Lannie inside.

"Okay, Lannie, what's up?"

"First, tell me about Mr. McHunky."

"That comes later. What's on your little mind?" I thought I knew.

"Guess who's here, Penelope?"

"I know. I saw him a few minutes ago. I had no idea he would come to the dance. Has he seen you? Have you talked to him?"

"Yeah, I saw him. Charley and Stella the Stinker made a point to come up to me and let me know they were here together. I was cool, Penelope. I smiled at both of them and told Charley it was nice to see him again. I lied through my teeth, of course. Then Thomas came over to save me by asking me to dance. That kid is the best. He told me not to worry, and that I'm better off without Charley. What really got to me is how protective he was of me, and that almost brought me to my knees. You should have seen him do the Polka!"

I saw tears glistening in her eyes. My heart was aching for her.

"But you know something, Penelope? I looked at Charley, really looked at him. He's a mess. I felt nothing for him, except maybe a little pity. It's just that Thomas the Lion was ready to do battle for me, and that was my undoing. All of a sudden I felt love all around me, and now I'm getting sappy and haven't even had anything to drink." Sniff, sniff.

I was getting sappy myself. "Come on, Lannie. Let's go party! You look like a million dollars. Let's go break a few hearts. In the words of my heroine, Scarlett, 'Tomorrow is another day.' And remember, we have a

volleyball game tomorrow, so we can break a few nails."
Oh, I'm sooo bad.

Faces freshly powdered, we entered the dance hall. I saw Derek standing with a group of my acquaintances and headed toward them, and Lannie took off toward the bar. I greeted my fellow shop owners. "Roger, Cathy, Herm, Lucy, how is everyone? Are you enjoying the dance?"

They all smiled their "hellos" and Roger answered, "We especially liked your rendition of the Polka. Never seen it done quite that way."

I took it like a big girl and smiled. I asked Lucy about her yarn shop, and we chatted for a bit about how knitting has become the new favorite hobby of both men and women. Herm asked me about my progress with the book.

Derek seemed surprised. "I didn't know you were writing a book. What's it about?"

"It's a murder mystery. I've always wanted to write a book, and now seems as good a time as any." I was hoping that we could talk about something else. I was getting nervous about my lack of progress with the storyline. Maybe I would work on it tomorrow after Mass, before going to the rec center.

"You are just full of surprises. I'm an Agatha Christie buff and have all of her books. Now I can start collecting the Penny Mitchell series. Come on, let's go eat, drink, and be merry. And I want to meet this brother of yours who made all the great food."

Chapter 5

"Miranda, I need your help. I can't do this alone. I don't know where we are or why we're here, but we have to pull together to get out of this mess. I understand how terrified you are of storms ever since you were locked in a basement during one when you were a kid. But you just have to get past that." Kevin couldn't see anything because of the total darkness. His hands and feet were bound, and he assumed that Miranda's were too. Why, he couldn't even do the Polka...

Time for a break. I couldn't seem to get last night out of my mind. Derek walked me to my car after the dance and gave me a sweet goodbye kiss. I couldn't believe how comfortable I felt with him after spending just a few hours in his company. He was inching his way into my heart. He told me all about his family. His parents live near Toledo, and his two brothers own a construction firm in Indianapolis. Derek told me that his family is the most important thing in his life, and they vacation together every year on Hilton Head Island during the last week in May. That is something we have in common: a love for our families. Hey, I've had relationships before, but I can't remember connecting with anyone this quickly. He didn't spend his time trying to impress me with his accomplishments. Derek used our time together to focus on me and learn about the things that are important to me. I am impressed with the total package.

"Come on, Tatters, let's go get ready for some V-ball. Ta-dada-ta-dada-ta-dada-ta-dada." I was humming the tune to *Rocky* to get myself mentally ready for the match. This game isn't for wimps. I didn't plop down big bucks for my new Jacuzzi for nothing. We play all-out, and I often come home bowed and bloody. I may have to rethink this sport in another fifteen or twenty years.

***

"That really wasn't very nice, Lannie. You could have broken her nose."

Lannie gave me her big-eyed puppy dog look. "I didn't mean to spike it into her face. I thought she would at least put her hands up. I took Stella at her word when she told me she was athletic. Anyway, jockettes don't run off the floor screeching that they'll need plastic surgery."

I hid a smile and silently chastised myself for being mean-spirited. Stella lasted a total of five minutes on the volleyball court, but it was a frustrating five minutes for me. She taunted the other team and kept whining when her own teammates wouldn't let her touch the ball. Every time someone did pass the ball to her she hit it with her knuckles, sending the ball flying off the court. Then disaster struck. My conscience kicked in, and I followed her to the ladies' locker room to offer what assistance I could, yelling over my shoulder to the other players to continue without me.

"Would you like me to walk you home, Stella?" I took a good look at her and cringed. Her nose and mouth were already considerably swollen, the tissue around her eyes showing signs of discoloration. Right now she looked like a cross between Jimmy Durante and Cher. By tomorrow she would look like a raccoon mauled by a bear.

"You an' dat fwiend of yours planned dis, and my nose is pwobably bwoken." Stella looked forlorn as she assessed the damage in the mirror. "Lannie is a bwute."

I could barely understand her, but got the gist of what she was saying. "I'm really sorry about this, Stella, but we always play hard, and thought that you were up to the challenge. If it's any consolation, I don't think your nose is broken. Look, the bleeding has stopped already. Let me walk you home. The swelling will go down as soon as you put some ice on it."

She gave me a dirty look, but allowed me to lead her from the locker room out the back door toward her house on Third Street, four blocks away from the recreation center. I pondered a moment, then asked her, partly out of curiosity and partly to distract her, "Stella, why is Charley back in town, and where is he staying?"

"I don' know why he's back. I saw him at Dick's Bar where we had a few dwinks and jus', you know, connected again. It was his idea to meet up at da dance. We went back to my house after an' had a few moe dwinks. He tol' me he was libbing in da Polson Building downtown."

I considered this information, then decided that the best way to find out anything was to go to Charley and ask him myself. I would have stayed out of it completely had Lannie not been involved. There had to be a reason for his reappearance in Columbus. He no longer had any family or friends here, as far as I knew. I'm not usually a suspicious person, but I could sense something was definitely wrong here, especially after the very strange conversations I overheard Charley having with Emile and Tony.

I got Stella situated, then went home to change out of my gym shorts and T-shirt and to think about how I was going to approach Charley. Tatters and I discussed the situation at length and came up with a plan. I've heard it said that it is prudent to keep one's enemies close, so I was going to pretend there was no bad blood between us and take him some goodies from my house to welcome him back. I would need to stop at the store to get a basket for my offerings. The Polson Building houses high-rise condominiums and is less than a mile from my house, just north of the Village on the other side of the freeway. I decided to drive since there is a parking lot adjacent to the building.

Less than an hour later I was in the lobby of the condo building, welcome basket in hand. I spotted the bank of mailboxes next to the elevators and scanned them for the name "Walker." There it was — Charles Walker, 7-E. I glanced around to make sure no one was paying any attention to me, entered an empty elevator car, and pushed the button for the seventh floor. The building is really quite beautiful with its ornately-decorated lobby and polished marble floors. The cost of these condos ranges from half a million to over a million dollars. I wondered how Charley could afford these prices. He was a Physical Education major in college and, after graduation, worked as an assistant manager in an athletic clothing store. Lannie had been the major breadwinner in the family, and that had really bothered Charley.

The elevator doors opened with a muted "ding," and I considered the wisdom of my actions. I figured that the worst that could happen would be for Charley to laugh in my face and slam the door. I took a deep breath and started down the hall toward 7-E, noting that my feet made virtually no noise on the plush carpet.

"That's odd," I thought to myself. The front door was ajar, so I could hear the noise of the TV set. "Why would Charley have the door open while he was watching TV?" I gave a little tap on the door and called, "Charley?" No answer. I pushed the door open a little wider to stick my head into the room. "Charley, are you here?" I called again. The living room of the condo was spacious, though sparsely furnished. I noted one lone couch against the far wall, angled to face the TV on an adjacent wall. There was a large picture window on the wall by the couch, but not much light came into the room because the blinds were drawn. I couldn't hear any noises from the bathroom or from anywhere else in the condo. I inched my body a little farther into the room and could see the kitchen area. From my vantage point, I could see two shoeless feet on the white-tiled kitchen floor, protruding onto the slate hallway. Those feet were not moving.

My ears were beginning to ring, and my body felt detached from my mind. I had felt this way once before. It was a hot July day about four years ago, temperatures hovering at one hundred degrees, and I was playing in a softball tournament. I was up at bat and got a good piece of the ball, enough to rocket it over the center fielder's head. I took off like a shot, rounded first base and, as I was heading for second, felt my mind detach from my body. I had enough sense to stop at second and plop myself down. My ears were ringing, and I saw lights flashing in front of my eyes, then nothing at all. The next thing I knew, I had opened my eyes to see a group of anxious faces staring down at me. Someone offered me a bottle of water, but I refused to remove my hands, still clutching second base, to grab the bottle. I reluctantly brought myself back to the present. I just knew that I didn't want to see who those feet belonged to.

I breathed slowly and deeply to steady myself, and took tiny little steps into the room whispering, "Charley?" I got closer and closer and could see that the legs attached to the feet were wearing khaki shorts that seemed to be stained with spaghetti sauce, and that the sauce had run down his legs and dripped on to the floor. Had Charley had an accident while cooking? Lord knows, that happens to me all the time. I looked a little higher at his head; that was a big mistake. Charley's face was almost unrecognizable due to all the blood that had come from the large dent in his forehead, and his eyes were staring sightlessly at the dishwasher. I groped my way backwards to the door and out to the corridor, pulling the door closed behind me. I tried taking deep breaths and slid down the wall, still clutching my welcome basket, into oblivion.

"Penelope! Penelope, what's wrong with you? Wake up! Come on, be a good girl." I could hear Lannie's voice, so I slowly opened my eyes, fighting nausea, trying to focus on her face. Lannie was kneeling next to me. "Are you hurt? You're as white as a sheet. What's wrong with you?"

"Lannie?" I mumbled. "What are you doing here?"

"I got an SOS call from Angela right after we finished the volleyball game, and she told me to find you, that it was important. There was no answer at your house, so I tried to call your cell, but your phone must have been turned off. I drove over to your store and saw you driving away, so I followed you. By the time I parked the car and got to the building the elevator doors were closing, and I saw the indicator stop at 7. I waited for the elevator to come back, got in, and pushed 7. The doors opened, and I saw you slumped on the floor. I thought you were dead!"

For once I blessed my mother's "radar." Lannie was here, so I didn't have to experience this nightmare alone. "Lannie, I h-have t-to tell you s-something." This wasn't going to be easy. Her ex-husband was dead just a few feet away, and I had to break the news. "Lannie," I grabbed her hand and squeezed. "Ch-Charley is in there" — I pointed to the door — "d-dead."

"Dead? Charley? What happened? Oh, God. What do you mean, dead? Tell me, Pen, what happened? Are you sure he's dead?"

"I'm pretty sure he's dead" — oh, yeah — "and I don't know what happened, Lannie. I brought him this welcome basket" — Lannie looked at the basket filled with soap balls, toilet paper, coupons, tomato soup, and a tape measure — "and I pushed the door open and saw him on the floor, dead."

Lannie jumped up to try the door, but it wouldn't open. It must have locked automatically when I pulled it shut.

"Lannie, we have to call the squad. Do you have your cell phone?"

Lannie grabbed her phone from her purse and punched in 9-1-1. We sat together in silence, waiting for help, just holding on to each other for comfort. I must have been in shock, because my memory of the ensuing events is sketchy. There was a flurry of frenetic activity, people running back and forth and talking into cell phones, and even more people arriving. Someone produced a key to unlock the door. I could hear muffled conversations from within Charley's unit. I know that Lannie got up to try to go in but was ushered out again and firmly told to wait in the hallway. A kind neighbor brought me a blanket because I was shivering uncontrollably, and someone else put a cup of strong, black coffee in my hands and told me to drink it.

Several police officers arrived with the squad crew, and several more arrived later. One of the policemen kept looking at Lannie and me and told us to "stay put" until someone could talk to us. I felt like a criminal. Time crawled by, or sped by, I don't remember. Lannie and I were still huddled together on the floor when I looked up and into the coldest, clearest, most serious case of gray eyes I had ever seen. It was as if those eyes could look into my soul and see every venial sin I had ever committed. I felt like lying on my back and exposing my jugular, conceding that he was, indeed, the alpha male in this situation.

"I'm Jack Sterling, CPD Homicide. I need to talk with you ladies. Come with me." We meekly followed him, on shaky legs, to an empty reception area at the end of the hall.

By then his words had registered. Lannie shouted, "Homicide! We don't need homicide! Charley's dead, but he hasn't been homicided, or whatever you call it."

He just gray-eyed her into silence. "Yes ladies, homicide. That man in there was bashed over the head and, I've been told, one of you found the body."

I couldn't think straight. My ears had started ringing again, and I was in danger of embarrassing everyone by throwing up on the beautiful plush carpet.

I asked inanely, "What does the 'C' stand for in CPD? You really should be more specific. It could be Cincinnati or Cleveland…"

Lannie nodded her head as if I made perfect sense and continued, "Or Chillicothe, Circleville…"

"Canton…"

He made a gesture with his hand that effectively stopped our ramblings. "Which one of you found the body?"

I slowly raised my hand parallel to my cheek, reminiscent of grade school. "I did." He waited. I rushed on. "You see, I was bringing Charley a welcome gift and I got to the door and the door was open and I stuck my head inside and I saw that he had an accident while he was cooking spaghetti and he was looking at the dishwasher and I was going to pass out and I had to go the hall and…"

Detective Sterling was losing patience. My mother always said I was intuitive, and I know these things. The fact that he was running his hand through his short-cropped dark hair and taking deep breaths reinforced my thoughts. He looked at my basket of offerings and asked, "Why were you bringing him soap, toilet paper, tomato soup and all that other stuff? Are you from Welcome Wagon?"

"No," I admitted. "Charley used to live around here and" — chuckle, chuckle — "he used to be married to Lannie. I just wanted to know what he was doing back in town and make sure he wasn't here to hurt Lannie. My idea was to bring him some gifts to soften him up for my interrogation." Lannie looked as if she wanted to disappear as Detective Sterling sent a fulminating glance her way.

"So you're the ex-wife, huh? Maybe you two had better come downtown with me and give me all the details. And just answer the questions I ask, okay?"

***

Lannie and I spent a long and exhausting day at the police station. The building itself is intimidating — all white marble, rising to an impressive height. I had never been to the station before and, I hope, never will be again. We were led to the sixth floor, where the homicide detectives have their offices. Signs warned us not to enter the area with any weapons. A cute little lady met us when the elevator door opened. I had her pegged as the department mascot because she looked to be about thirteen and had the most innocent blue eyes I had ever seen, except for Mom's. She was crisply efficient-looking in beige slacks and a celery-green linen blazer worn over a cream-colored shell. Detective Sterling had ridden up on the elevator with us and introduced us to the lady.

"Ms. Mitchell and Ms. Daugherty, I would like you to meet my colleague, Detective Erin Kelly."

Our jaws dropped. This little sprite could not be a big, bad homicide detective!

Lannie and I looked at each other in disbelief, much to the amusement of Detective Sterling.

He and Erin exchanged a smile that suggested that this had happened on more than one occasion. He explained, "Erin is just back from maternity leave and has four little boys at home. Believe me, she can handle the most desperate of criminals. I know because I've met her kids. And she holds the department record for being the best marksman on the squad."

Detective Kelly smiled and said, "Nice to meet you." She took a closer look at Lannie and asked, "Are you the Ms. Daugherty who teaches English at North High School?"

Lannie nodded her head and looked bewildered that Erin Kelly knew about her. Did Lannie have a rap sheet or something? Was her poster on the post office's wall?

Detective Kelly clasped Lannie's hands in her own and said, "You literally saved my little brother's life. Eric Seaburn, that's my brother, was in your class about four years ago and, at the time, was hanging out with a bad crowd and starting to get into trouble at school."

Lannie's smile was genuine as she repeated, "Eric Seaburn."

"It was just a matter of time before things got more serious. My family and I just about went nuts trying to straighten him out, but he wouldn't listen to us. I don't know what you said or did, but you took an interest in him and helped him out. He is in his last year at the University of Cincinnati, majoring in Mechanical Engineering, and has a wonderful girl-friend. The future looks bright for Eric. I can't ever thank you enough."

Lannie was sincerely delighted to hear about Eric and his success. "I remember him fondly, and I'm glad he's doing so well. I really didn't do anything extraordinary. I just pointed out some facts to him. Kids will sometimes listen to an outsider much more readily than their own families."

"Well, I'm eternally grateful." Erin Kelly glanced at Detective Sterling and said, "Jack, you be nice to this lady and her friend." Then she whispered to Lannie, "I hope you didn't do it." She wished us luck and headed off to the equipment room to check the sound levels and the taping apparatus.

Detective Sterling led us back to the interrogation room, which was approximately the size of a large box, and apologized for the inconvenience. Our grade school training with the nuns surfaced as we both said, "Oh, no, it's okay."

I was proud of the way Lannie kept her composure under Detective Sterling's intense scrutiny. Everyone in that little interrogation room knew that the spouse, or in this case the ex-spouse, is statistically the most likely to commit the crime. I was next in line, since I found the body. He made us repeat our timeline for the day about a thousand times. After about four hours of this, Lannie started giggling when she got to the part about smashing Stella in the face with the volleyball. I made the mistake of looking at her and lost all control. We were practically rolling on the floor with laughter. Jack Sterling was not amused. He raised his chiseled jaw, narrowed those steely eyes, and said, "I think you're crazy."

Lannie exploded, while I cowered in my chair. "I'm not crazy, just a little reality challenged, okay? I've had a tough day. Charley may have been a dastard, but I-did-not-kill-him! ¿Comprende?"

"Dastard?" Detective Sterling repeated with a startled expression.

"My mother won't let her cuss," I explained.

I could tell that the man had reached his limit for the day. He sat completely still and breathed in and out for a few minutes. "Okay you two, go home."

Lannie declined my offer of company when we left, saying she needed to be by herself to think for a while. We were both shaken when Detective Sterling told us not to leave town, and that he would probably come looking for us tomorrow to ask more questions.

Lannie hugged me outside the police station and said, "I hope you don't think I'm selfish for wanting to be alone right now. I just need to stare at my walls for a while and absorb all that has happened. This may take some time to process."

"Of course you're not selfish! You need to take care of yourself right now in any way that works for you. It's like being on an airplane. The flight attendants always tell the mothers to take care of their own oxygen masks before tending to their children. You just go on home now and do what you need to do."

Lannie smiled weakly and turned toward her car. I felt so sorry for her and hoped we would both be able to get some sleep tonight.

***

Tatters ran to meet me when I walked in the front door. "I bet your bladder is about to burst, little guy."

I heard my mother's voice from the kitchen. "He just went out, Penny darling, and I'm here to baby you. I sent Taylor and Thomas over to the store to get the fixings for dinner."

"Oh, God," I thought, "I hope we're not having spaghetti." At that idea my lips started to tremble, and I could feel the tears well up in my eyes. Mom came toward me and hugged me.

"Everything will be okay, sweetie. Your family is going to take care of you. You can come home with us later and spend the night if you want to."

Kindness is always my undoing. I can stand anything, but someone being kind to me makes me cry. Mom led me to the couch, sat me down, and held me while I had a good purging. I told my story yet again in fits and starts. Taylor and Thomas returned with the groceries, and Mom disappeared into the kitchen while I told the kids what had happened. I felt much better with each telling. I had a fleeting thought of me walking up and down my street, knocking on doors, and begging my neighbors to listen to my story.

I really did feel considerably better after Mom's comfort food. We enjoyed a reasonable semblance of a normal meal with tacos, Mom's famous salsa and chips, and a fresh salad. I managed to eat a fair amount while listening to Taylor and Thomas prattle on about the talent show, their new jobs, and the laundromat project. After dinner, Taylor and I went to the den to watch

Jeopardy while Mom and Thomas did the cleanup. Taylor and I were neck and neck until I beat her in final jeopardy. The category was Geography, not my strong point, but I bet my entire twenty-five thousand dollars.

Alex Trebek read, "This is the highest mountain peak in all of the Americas." I almost let victory slip through my fingers as I thought about Alaska. At the last possible moment I got it.

Taylor answered, "What is Mt. McKinley?"

I smiled wickedly and said, "What is Aconcagua?" — a mountain peak in the Andes chain. Not one of the contestants got it right.

Finally, Alex said, in that serious way of his, "The correct answer is…Aconcagua!"

I did a little victory dance, and Mom and Thomas came to the door of the den to see what all the excitement was about.

"I just won fifty thousand dollars and am the champion of the universe!"

Mom smiled and said, "I'm glad you're feeling better."

I patted her on her little head and said, "Thanks, Mom. I do feel better, and I'm sure I'm going to be okay tonight. Tatters will take care of me. I am a little worried about Lannie, though. Could you stop by her place on your way home and take her some tacos and some of that delicious salsa? And maybe make her cry, too? That helped me out."

Mom and the kids thought that would be a good idea, and packed up their belongings to head over to Lannie's. They all shouted "hasta la vista" as they went out the front door. I watched them leave and then went upstairs for a long, hot bath. I would get up early to do some writing before going to the shop. I had to try to carry on as normal an existence as possible. I would not let any horrible thoughts enter into my head. I just hoped my unconscious mind was as resolute.

Chapter 6

By working together as a team, Kevin and Miranda were making progress freeing themselves from their bindings. Kevin was so very proud that Miranda had pulled herself together. He knew that their salvation would stem from action.

"Miranda, as soon as my hands are free I'll try to feel my way around the perimeter of the room. Maybe there is a door or a blacked-out window..."

I decided to take Tatters to the shop with me today in case I needed a hug. Paula and Andy might not understand if I suddenly threw myself on them. I did get some sleep last night, but it was intermittent, and today I felt a little dopey. The details on the morning news were very sketchy, but the police did release the victim's name.

Paula met me at the door of the shop. "Penny, did you hear the news that Charley Walker was murdered?"

"Unfortunately, I know all about it." I shocked them both with my story, and appreciated the concern on their faces as they listened intently to the whole sordid tale.

Andy put his arm around my shoulder and asked, "Are you sure you want to work today? Paula and I can handle the customers, and Alice is due in this afternoon. There is no need for you to be here if you'd rather be home."

I was touched. "No, it really is better for me to have something to do. If I stayed home, I would keep going over it and over it. Trust me, I need to be here."

Every customer in the shop that morning wanted to talk about the murder. Charley Walker was known around the Village, if not in person at least by reputation, even though he had been gone for seven years. The population of German Village is only about 4,000 people, and many of them have been residents for years. It's hard to have any secrets in such a small community. Lannie's breakup and divorce were common knowledge. Lannie moved from Grandview, a lovely little community west of downtown Columbus, to Beck Street in the Village immediately after the punching incident. Lannie is well-respected and well-liked. Everyone was supportive of her after she left Charley, and welcomed her into the community.

Paula went to the back of the shop to brew some coffee for a mid-morning break while Andy ran to the bank to make some deposits. Tatters and I were alone for the time being. I decided to dust some displays and let my mind wander. I find that if I don't think about anything at all, my problems sort of work themselves to the surface and take care of themselves. I was deep in "nowhere land" when I heard the jangle of the door opening. I turned and saw Bob, our mailman. I was caught! Bob's one claim to fame is that Wilt Chamberlain was his uncle, which I seriously doubt. Bob stands about five-six on a good day, and that is at the beginning of his route. What he lacks in height he more than makes up for with an overly developed mouth. That man can talk! I try to avoid the niceties when Bob's around because a simple "how are you?" can easily stretch into a twenty-minute answer. Neither rain, nor sleet... but a willing ear will stop him dead in his tracks. I honestly don't know how he finishes his daily deliveries before midnight. Tatters was delighted to see Bob and jumped up and down. He knows that Bob carries dog biscuits in his pocket just in case he needs to tame some savage beast on his route. Tatters took his treat and ran behind the counter so I wouldn't steal it. I gave Bob a tepid smile and a luke-warm "hello." I tried to look really, really busy, but Bob was having none of that.

"Good morning, Penny. Hey, did you hear the news? Everybody is talking about it."

"Well, Bob, I..." Just then the phone rang. Gratefully, I scooped it up. "Whimsies, this is Penny. How may I help you?" It was a wrong number, but I continued talking to the dial tone, hoping that Bob would give up and leave.

Just then, Lannie came into the store carrying a Full of Beans coffee cup. She greeted Bob, and they spoke in low tones so they wouldn't disturb my important call. I heard her tell him about finding the body. I could tell that she had had a rough night. Dark smudges were visible under her eyes, and her eyes were lacking their usual sparkle. There was a flatness in her expression that I hadn't seen since her days with Charley. I had a momentary flash of anger at Charley, then instantly regretted it. No matter what he had done in his life, he didn't deserve to die that way. I resolved right then and there to try to find out who had murdered him. Maybe then Lannie could find peace and closure for that episode of her life. Bob murmured something about how he had lost someone in a horrible way, so he could sympathize with her. He patted her on the shoulder and left the shop.

"Hi, Penelope, I see you're still doing the old phone trick." I never could fool Lannie. "I just came from your paramour's shop. Derek is all set for the grand opening tomorrow. I sort of filled him in on yesterday's events; he's really worried about you. He told me to tell you that he'd be over in a little bit, just as soon as he and Max finish setting up the displays and his deliveries arrive."

I smiled at Lannie while a collage of images flitted through my mind: Lannie and I ready to make our first communion, when she let out a big burp, making the entire congregation laugh; the time she fell into the water at Mackin's Pond and a mother duck, quacking furiously, chased her out, biting her on the butt; the day I fell off my bike and skinned both knees, and Lannie let me lean on her all the way home; Lannie personally spear-heading a fundraiser after my father's death to have a statue of St. Jude (his favorite saint) placed in the vestibule of the church with a plaque that read "In Loving Memory of Joseph Patrick Mitchell." You just had to love a girl like that.

"Hi, Lannie. Sorry you got stuck with Bob...I just wasn't up to it. Tell me, how are you doing today?"

"Pretty good, actually. I felt better after Angela and the twins came over with their food offerings and sympathetic shoulders. I cried like a baby and felt one hundred percent better for it. I called Mom and Dad in Florida, and they offered to fly up here to give me moral support, but I told them to stay put. They were reluctant to do that, until I solemnly promised to call them every day to let them know what's happening."

"Mom will probably call Larry and Ann and tell them the exact same thing. So...you saw Derek this morning, huh?"

"Yeah, and now I know why his dog is named Loretta. She looks just like Loretta Young."

Lannie and I have a Friday Night Classic Film Fest at least once a month where we watch old movies, eat popcorn, and laugh and cry to our hearts' content. We take turns hosting it, often inviting other friends or family members. One of our favorites is *The Bishop's Wife* with Loretta Young, David Niven, and Cary Grant. Other movies in the running are: *Wizard of Oz*, *Dial M for Murder*, *Midnight Lace*, and *African Queen*. Topping the list of our best scary movies are *Jaws* and the original *Halloween*. Our all-time favorite, though, is *Groundhog Day*. We love the part where weatherman Phil Connors (played by Bill Murray) kidnaps Punxsutawney Phil (played by Scooter) and roars off in a red pickup truck. Scooter's character is sitting on the lap of Bill Murray's character helping to steer the truck and is warned, "Don't drive angry." That always cracks us up. Every time one of us gets in a car, the other says, "Don't drive angry."

"Lannie, why don't you come over tonight to watch *Groundhog Day*? You know it always puts us in a good mood. It's the best movie ever made and sure to be a classic some day."

"Good idea, Penelope, and I promise not to 'drive angry.' Back to Derek... he really seems like a nice guy. Tell me more about him."

"Well, I've only spent a few hours with him and" —I ticked his good points on my fingers — "he's really nice to my family, he loves his own family, he treats Loretta like a princess, and he's a good dancer, except for the Polka." We both grinned at that one.

"Sounds like a winner to me. I only spent a few minutes with him at Full of Beans, but he was genuinely concerned about both of us and sincere in his offer to help us out. He wanted to run right over, but had to wait on an important delivery. If you want to go over there, I'll watch the store for a bit."

"Thanks, Lannie, but Paula and Andy are here today. I'll…"

The door jangled open, and we turned to watch Stella clickety-click over to the counter. Daylight was not kind to her bruised and battered face. Her expression was dour, and there was an evil gleam in her eye. If this had been the Old West, I would have had her check her holster at the door.

"Good morning, Stella, you're looking lovelier than ever," Lannie said sweetly. I shot her a look that said, loud and clear, to knock it off.

"Look what you two did to me! I have to meet with clients today, and I'll probably lose business because of you." Tatters came out from behind the counter, licking his chops. He took one look at Stella and began to growl. Tatters has good taste; he can't stand Stella.

"Just a minute, Stella." Lannie's voice lost its sweetness and became very soft. I imagine that is how she talks to her uncooperative students. "We didn't *do* anything to you. It was an accident. Anyway, you were the one who wanted to play with the big girls. It's always about you, isn't it? There has been a murder of a man we all know, and all you can think about is yourself. I know

76

you had a relationship with Charley. Don't you even have one little thought for him today?" Lannie jabbed her finger in Stella's direction.

Stella puffed herself up and prepared to answer. "How dare…"

The door jangled again as Detective Sterling came into the shop. I inwardly groaned. Things were going from bad to worse. Paula walked into the customer area from the back room, glanced around the room, grabbed Tatters, and disappeared again. I wanted to go with them. Stella's expression mellowed as she gave Detective Sterling the once-over.

"How do you do? I'm Stella Morgan and you're…?"

"Detective Jack Sterling, CPD."

Lannie deadpanned, "The 'C' stands for Columbus."

Detective Sterling ignored her and addressed Stella. "What happened to you?"

Stella wore a smug expression as she pointed to Lannie and me. "They beat me up."

Jack Sterling shot us a startled look. Lannie rolled her eyes and swore under her breath. I started to protest, then thought better of it. I didn't want to sound defensive.

"I need to talk with all of you. Ms. Mitchell and Ms. Daugherty, will you be available in about an hour? We can talk here if you'd like. Is there an office available for our conference?"

I liked how he used the word "conference" as a euphemism for "interrogation." "Yes, there is an office in the back we can use. Now is a good time if it works for you."

"Let's make it in an hour. Ms. Morgan, could you accompany me now? There are a few questions I'd like you to answer."

Stella appeared to be uncertain. I could tell that she was itching to get Detective Sterling alone to work her magic on him, but she didn't like the idea of being perceived as a suspect. Her hormones won out.

"My office is just down the block, detective." Stella was actually purring. "Let's go there so we can have some privacy." She grabbed his arm and leaned into him, steering him out the door. She shot a smug look over her shoulder at Lannie and me.

"I can't believe her! She's acting like they are going out on a date." Lannie stood there shaking her head. "I actually feel pity for the man." She glanced at her watch. "Okay, I've got an hour. I'm going to run some errands and grab a sandwich. Do you want me to bring something back for you from the Mohawk?"

The Old Mohawk is one of Columbus's best eating places, located in the Village a block from my shop. Their sandwiches are legendary. I usually eat there three or four times a week. Monday night is "fried chicken night," and I was planning to have dinner there.

"No thanks, Lannie. I brought a sandwich from home and a puzzle to do over lunch." Tatters and I love to spend our lunch time doing the *Columbus Dispatch* crossword puzzle. It helps to keep our minds sharp and our spirits up. "You go do your stuff, and I'll see you in a bit."

Time passed quickly as the customers poured in. I was busy answering questions and ringing up merchandize. My favorite part of the day is interacting with people, and I love to hear their compliments about the shop. Some live in the Village, but the vast majority come from out of town. It's not uncommon to see chartered buses lining the streets, bringing in sightseers who are enjoying a day trip to German Village.

"Paula, I'm taking my lunch break now. Call me from the back if you need me." I got my sandwich and a bottle of iced tea from the mini-fridge. I settled at the little table in the office, opening the paper to the puzzle section and munching on my turkey sandwich. Tatters was dining on his mini-chunks. I can't break him of his bad habit of playing with his food. He takes each pellet of food from his bowl and pushes it around the floor, sits and watches it for a while, then pounces. I was just finishing my lunch and pondering a particularly baffling clue when the door opened. Derek peeked in the room.

"Paula told me you were back here. Is it okay to come in?"

"Sure. Come on in. Have you eaten yet?" I couldn't help the big grin. Just seeing him made me feel so much better.

"I had lunch while I was waiting for the cappuccino machine to be delivered, thanks. Lannie told me what happened yesterday, and I feel just terrible. Are you okay?"

"I'm going to be fine. I still can't believe it happened... it's surreal. I'll go for a while and forget about finding Charley, and then it all comes back to me. Talking about it really helps."

"Would you like to have dinner with me tonight? You could talk all you want, and I promise not to interrupt."

"I would like that very much. I was planning to go to the Old Mohawk tonight for their fried chicken. Care to join me?"

"Great. I've been meaning to try it out. A lot people have suggested that restaurant, along with about a dozen more. It's going to take me months to eat my way through German Village." He glanced at the newspaper. "Are you stuck on a clue?"

I hated to admit that I was. I feel like a failure if I can't solve the entire puzzle, but what's worse is leaving a space empty. It ruins the symmetry of life. I swallowed my pride and nodded.

"What's the clue?"

"I need an eight letter word for what a balalaika player is."

Derek thought for a moment and answered, "Strummer."

Of course! I knew that I could have figured it out if I had just given myself some time. I wrote it in the spaces (I'm a professional, so I use a pen) and then looked at Derek, narrowing my eyes. Okay, Mr. Hotshot, how about this one? I smiled sweetly and asked, "How about a four letter word for cup holder?"

He took the challenge and looked me straight in the eye. "Zarf. Five letter word for shoelace tip," he shot right back at me.

I stared off into space and bit my lower lip, waiting for enlightenment. Aha! "Aglet."

"I concede that you are an expert. Do you like to do the Sunday *New York Times* puzzle?"

"If I could, I would love to stay in bed all morning and work on it. I have a standing game of volleyball on Sunday mornings after Mass, so I work on the puzzle throughout the day. I have to admit that I don't usually get all the answers. How about you?"

"Me either, but I never stop trying. We should work on it together sometime."

Very interesting possibilities here! I was considering how to answer him when Paula stuck her head through the door to tell me I had company. I knew exactly who my "company" was, and was dreading the encounter.

"Derek, do you want to meet over at the Mohawk about six o'clock? I'm off at four today, and that will give me time to take Tatters home and work on my book for a while. I have to be home by eight, though, because Lannie is coming over to watch a movie."

"Perfect. That will give me time to get back to the store and do a few minor things before we open tomorrow. See you then, Penny. Feel free to call me anytime if you need me."

What a guy! I was looking forward to seeing him again and gorging myself on fried chicken, mashed potatoes, and corn on the cob. I was not looking forward to my upcoming interview with Detective Sterling. To tell the truth, he scared the poop out of me. Every time he turned those steely-gray eyes in my direction, I felt like throwing myself at his feet and confessing to every little crime I ever committed in my life. I had a vision of myself tearfully begging for mercy for the time I put an empty envelope into the collection basket at church. I was only eight, but I knew better. Part of my weekly allowance of one dollar was designated to go to the poor orphans, but I got greedy and kept the whole amount to buy chocolate to feed my habit. I wondered about the statute of limitations on defrauding the Church and figured I was safe for now.

I told Tatters he was not welcome at the interview, although I was tempted to let him stay for moral support. I stood up, took a deep breath and, as bravely as possible, opened the door and invited Detective Sterling in while ushering Tatters out. Tatters, the traitor, wagged his tail and stood grinning at the detective. That dog is shameless. I saw the smile that transformed the detective's face and felt for the first time that everything might just turn out all right. Paula came to the door to grab Tatters and sent me an encouraging look.

"Cute dog. What kind is he?"

"He's a Yorkie-Poodle mix, and he has the best temperament in the world."

"I used to have a Boxer named Ali when I was a little boy. I loved that dog."

I tried to imagine Detective Sterling as a little boy and failed. I thought that he must be a decent human being if he liked Tatters. I considered my strategy for the interview and decided to try to act as normally as possible.

"Come and sit here, Detective Sterling." I gestured to an empty chair at the table. "Can I offer you some iced tea or a soft drink?"

"No thanks, I just had lunch. Where is your friend? She was supposed to be here."

Just as he said the words there was a perfunctory knock on the door. Lannie poked her head through the opening and asked, "Am I late?"

"No," we both answered in unison.

I deferred to Detective Sterling. "We're just getting started. Come on in."

Lannie sauntered in and opened the refrigerator door before having a seat. She chose a soft drink and took her time getting situated. She sent an insolent look toward Detective Sterling and said, "Well?"

To his credit, he didn't take the bait. "Ladies, thank you for making yourselves available to help us out. We can't do this alone, and any information you can give us is appreciated. First of all, I'd like you to know that the body will probably be released tomorrow or Wednesday."

Lannie started to speak, but Detective Sterling anticipated her question. "The body is to be released to an aunt who lives in Colorado. Mr. Walker's mother died two years ago, and the aunt is his only living relative. She wants to bury Mr. Walker next to his mother."

Lannie and I looked at each other, and I could see the pain in her eyes. Lannie truly cared for Edna Walker. That lady was a saint! She was always kind to Lannie and treated her like a daughter. I don't think Edna was aware of how badly Charley treated Lannie, at least at the beginning of the marriage. When Lannie filed for divorce, Edna went to see her to tell her that she was ashamed of Charley, and that she had done her best to raise him. "All I can say, Lannie, is that he is a bad seed. His father and I did our best. We even took Charley to see our pastor, hoping maybe he could influence the boy to be better. Nothing worked. That boy is incapable of love, and I thank you for giving him a fair chance. You were good for him, and I hoped he would turn around. I don't know what will happen now that I'm moving to Colorado to be near my sister, Linda. He is in God's hands now. You take care, Lannie, and get on with your life."

"Thanks for letting us know that," whispered Lannie. Then she lifted her eyes and looked straight at the detective. "I just want to say something up front. I know I'm the most likely suspect" — Lannie sent me a warning glare when I nodded my head — "but I swear to you I did not kill Charley. I'll admit that my life with him was not a walk in the rose garden; it was more like running through the briar patch — naked." She held up her hand as he started to speak. "The only time I've seen Charley during the past seven years was at the dance on Saturday, and we only exchanged a few words. There, that's it. Finito. Shouldn't you be out browbeating other suspects or investigating the crime scene or something?"

Wow. I was amazed that Lannie didn't seem the least bit intimidated by Detective Sterling. The air was crackling with tension. I could see the muscle twitching in his cheek as he fought back a retort. Being in the same room as those two was like being in the ring with two boxers as they danced around each other waiting to throw a knock-out punch. I was getting a headache. "Lannie, be nice. Detective Sterling is only trying to do his job and doesn't really suspect you of anything." I glanced toward him. "Right?"

"To be perfectly honest, I can't rule out anyone at this stage. That's why I'm gathering all the information I can, and you could really help me out by being more cooperative."

Lannie opened her mouth for yet another comeback, but Paula interrupted her by opening the door. "Penny, P.J. is out here and wants to see you for a minute." I jumped up, grateful to get away for a few moments, and told the two of them I would be right back.

I took a deep breath as I closed the door behind me, and wondered if they would tear my office apart if I left them alone. I spotted P.J. sitting on his heels, scratching Tatters behind the ears. I tried to compose my face as I approached him, but he knows me too well. The instant he rose to hug me I burst into tears, shocking the customers who were browsing in the shop. "I'm just so happy to see him," I explained. "Don't forget that the red-tagged items have an additional ten-percent discount."

I grabbed P.J. by the hand and dragged him out the front door where we could have a little privacy.

"Whew, I thought I was doing so well! One look at your ugly face and I'm a blubbering idiot."

P.J. remained serious. "Pen, I was going to ask if you were okay, but it's obvious you're not. Mom told me what happened, and I'm absolutely astounded. Grace and I want you to come and stay at our house"— I started to shake my head — "No, hear me out. You need to be near family now, at least until you have a little time and distance to get over the trauma of finding a body, let alone someone you knew. We promise to treat you like a princess and wait on you hand and foot. I take a solemn oath" — he raised his right hand and mimicked putting his left on a Bible — "not to read your diary or put G.I. Joe clothes on your Barbie."

I giggled at the memory, while trying to wipe my eyes and blow my nose. "Mom offered, too. I really appreciate it, Peej. You and Grace are really sweet to want to help out, but I will be fine. Listen, I have to get back in there. I left Lannie alone with a policeman, and I fear for his safety." P.J. knows Lannie as well as I do, and he gave me a smile. "I know you have to go to work now, so I'll call Grace later on to check in. Please don't worry about me, okay? By the way, what's the Chef's Special tonight?"

"Sole Almondine. I know I can't compete with the Mohawk on Monday nights, but why don't you bring your new boyfriend to the restaurant some time this week and I'll make your favorite." I let the comment about the "boyfriend" pass, and thought about P.J.'s incomparable pot roast.

"You're on. And, Peej, thanks for being a good brother."

After P.J. left I stood outside for a bit, trying to compose myself. The sky was clouding over with the threat of a thunder storm. The weather was matching my mood. My sense of civic duty kicked in, so I went back in to face the law and continue our "conference." I had my hand on the doorknob to the office when it hit me that there was no screaming coming from inside. In fact, it was ominously quiet. Standing outside of doors and listening to conversations was getting to be a bad habit, but I was perfecting the technique. No one from the shop was paying any attention to me. The office is accessible through a small hallway from the shop, so if I stood in the shadows I wasn't too noticeable. I could have used a potted palm, though. I couldn't hear anything, so I turned the handle to crack the door.

"Come in, Penelope. The reason you can't hear anything is that we are not talking."

Darn! Lannie didn't always have to be so blunt. "I was just coming in slowly so I wouldn't startle you." I don't think either of them bought my explanation. "Okay, where were we?" I asked brightly to cover my discomfiture.

Detective Sterling looked at me and said, "Ms. Mitchell, I would appreciate it if you would tell me again about finding the body. Sometimes small details escape a witness that will surface later. At least he called me a "witness" instead of a "perpetrator."

I bowed to the inevitable and began my timetable for yesterday. Was it just yesterday? It seemed so long ago, and my memory was already dimming. I could understand why Detective Sterling was so anxious for us to recount all the details while they were still fresh in our minds. I came to the part where I walked in the door and discovered the body. All of a sudden I stopped. Both Lannie and Detective Sterling leaned forward in their chairs.

"What is it, Ms. Mitchell? Do you remember something?"

"Yeah, Penelope, what gives?"

I put my elbows on the table and my face in my hands. After a few seconds, I looked up and admitted, "Yes, I guess I saw something that I failed to mention before."

They both cocked their heads, just like Tatters does when he's waiting for me to say something.

"I remember that Charley was lying on his back, maybe tilted a little toward his left side, with his right arm slung over his chest. He…he may have been trying to write something in his own blood." I gave an involuntary shudder and stood up to move around. "It looked like a capital 'P' or 'D,' but the curved line was incomplete. It just sort of ended right after the curved part."

Lannie groaned, and I got busy examining my fingernails. Detective Sterling smiled a predatory kind of smile and said, "I'm glad you remembered that little detail. I was wondering if you would mention it or not."

Lannie said, "That's so lame, Penelope. That kind of stuff only happens in third-rate novels."

Hmm. Maybe I could use it in my book.

I suddenly brightened. "Hey, it could have been a 'B' or a lower case 'r'."

Lannie joined in, "Or a lower case 'n' or 'm'."

Detective Sterling almost yelled. "Enough. The lab boys have plenty of pictures, and we are trained to consider all the configurations."

Configurations. I was impressed. "Do you like to work on puzzles? My personal goal is to complete the *New York Times* puzzle in less than two hours."

It was Detective Sterling's turn to groan and put his head in his hands. "Tell me," he lifted his eyes to meet mine and asked, "are you two always like this when you get together?"

Lannie and I smiled at each other and she answered, "Penny's father used to tell us that we were enough to drive any man crazy. When we get nervous or excited we tend to babble. We make perfect sense to each other, but I guess other people find it kind of hard to follow along." Lannie's demeanor softened at the memory of my father. "Detective Sterling, I promise to be nice from now on." He looked surprised. "I really don't have a mean bone in my body — well, maybe one or two metacarpals — and Penny is as sweet as they come. It's just not in us to kill anybody; I have been rotten because this whole situation has just floored me. I apologize."

"She's right, Detective Sterling. This is the first time we have ever been involved in a...uh...police investigation. And Lannie is even sweeter than I am. In fact, she is so sweet she has been known to cause cavities."

"Oh, Penelope, I'm going to cry."

Jack Sterling's normally inscrutable face underwent an amazing transformation. His expression went from shell-shocked, to baffled, to sympathetic. He didn't look like a big, bad policeman anymore.

"Okay, ladies. I know this has been hard on you. Being involved in a murder investigation is traumatic for most people; hardly anyone has experience with this type of thing. I don't really consider you suspects — that's off the record, by the way — because the forensic evidence tends to exclude you. But, that doesn't mean that I don't need your help to solve this case."

"Why didn't you…"

I knew Lannie was going to lambaste him for not mentioning this a whole lot earlier, so I quickly came up with something to derail her.

"For the record, Detective Sterling, we didn't beat up Stella. She just stuck her face in the path of a speeding volleyball. Lannie's fist may have been on the other end of that speeding volleyball, but it was an accident."

"That's right, sir. She told us she could play," Lannie giggled, "but you should have seen her. She did a few pirouettes on the court and… and" — Lannie was losing it fast — "t-tried to…jump…over the…b-ball." Lannie clutched at her stomach and started to laugh in earnest.

I joined right in and was surprised to see Detective Sterling take out his handkerchief and pretend to wipe his brow. I guess, having spent some time with her, he knew Stella well enough to appreciate the story.

We all finally composed ourselves, and Detective Sterling excused himself to go do whatever homicide investigators do. Lannie also got up to leave and paused. "What forensic evidence do you think he was talking about?"

"I don't know for sure, Lannie, but I've been thinking about this. If I look at this like a puzzle it doesn't bother me so much, and I might be able to figure out part of it. Are you sure you want to hear this?"

Lannie nodded her head and said, "I'll look at it like a puzzle, too. That way we can be of some help to the CPD." She gave me her most devilish smile.

"The way I see it, whoever bashed Charley on the head had to have gotten blood splatter on his or her clothing."

"His or her?"

"Yeah, it could have been a woman. Hmm..." I drummed my fingers on the table, deep in thought. "Let me think about this for awhile, and we'll talk some more when you come over tonight, okay? I'm having dinner with Derek tonight, but I promise to be home in time for the movie."

Lannie gave me wink and said, "Have a good time."

Chapter 7

"Miranda, there is something on the floor over here, and it's soft. Good God, I think it's a body!" Kevin had to make a conscious effort not to let the nausea overtake him. He took a couple of deep breaths and willed himself not to panic.

"Do you mean a human body?" Miranda was practically screeching.

"I don't know, Miranda. Stay calm, we'll figure this out. I'm going to try to find a pulse." Kevin fought against his revulsion to touch the body. He tentatively ran his hand over the body to find a pulse point. He touched skin and automatically shrank away from the sticky wetness...

"You be a good boy, Tatters, and guard the house while I'm away. If you're really good, I promise to let you have a piece of popcorn when Lannie comes over."

Tatters jumped up and down. I swear he understands every word I say. He is into immediate gratification, and didn't want to wait until later. I broke down and gave him a little piece of cheese to hold him off; I don't understand why I let him manipulate me.

I got to the Mohawk about five minutes early. Grandma Mitchell says that it's better to arrive one hour early than one minute late, and I have always taken her advice to heart. I opened the door and greeted Clint, the manager.

"Hi, Clint. There will be two of us for dinner tonight."

"Hey, Penny, what's up? Your mom and the twins are over by the window. Do you want to join them?"

I glanced over and saw Mom and the kids chatting away with Derek.

"No, Clint. We'll want our own table, maybe over there." I pointed to the far side of the restaurant.

"Sure thing, Penny. Give me a minute to clear a table. Sara will be your waitress. Enjoy!"

I walked toward my little family unit and gave an involuntary smile. Thomas was busy stuffing his face, and Taylor and Derek were deep in conversation. Mom looked adorable with her hair in a ponytail and sparkly pink flip-flops on her little feet. She was enjoying a glass of merlot and smiling at her offspring. I could hear Taylor asking Derek what time they should report to work tomorrow.

"Why don't you guys come about eight-thirty? That will give me time to go over some of the finer details with you before the big crowd hits at nine."

Taylor said, "Okay, Derek. We are really excited, and you won't be sorry you hired us."

Thomas nodded and continued eating. He saw me coming and gave a little wave. The rest of them turned toward me and smiled their "hellos."

"Hi! I should have figured that everyone would be here tonight. See how popular this place is on a Monday night, Derek?"

"Hi, Penny. I'm so glad you suggested this place. I love the ambiance, and can't wait to sample the food.

Thomas is a good advertisement for the Mohawk. This is his third plate of food."

"Buenas tardes, Penny. La comida es sabrosa, como siempre."

"Hola, Mamacita. I'm glad you're enjoying it. I hope you don't mind if I steal Derek. I promised him a delicious meal and to fill him in on the last twenty-four hours."

"Go for it, Penny. Are you sure you're doing all right? Taylor and Thomas begged me to let them come to the shop today, but I thought you would be busy answering questions from all of your regulars."

"You're right, Mom, as usual. Everybody and his brother wanted to know the details of the…er…crime." I smiled at Taylor and Thomas. "You kids are so sweet to worry about me, but please don't. I'm really okay. P.J. stopped by to check on me, and I spent some time today with Lannie. She's doing just fine. Thanks for going over to her place last night. She really appreciated it.

"Ningún problema."

"Sure, Pen, we were happy to help. Vivimos para servir."

Derek looked concerned at the mention of the murder, so I sent him a reassuring smile.

"Our table is ready now. Mom, I'll call you tomorrow. Taylor and Thomas, break a couple of legs at work tomorrow, and don't take any baloney from your boss. I'm coming over during my break tomorrow morning, and I'm expecting exemplary service."

Thomas said between mouthfuls, "Penny, you are going to be amazed at how professional Taylor and I are going to be. Hasta mañana."

As Derek and I were making our way toward the table he said, "I've got one for you, Penny. What's a six letter word for grudge?"

Hmm. "Give me a hint. What does it start with?"

"A"

"Got it. Animus. Here's one for you. Since we're on the letter 'a', a three letter word for a black cuckoo."

"Penny, you are too kind. Ani."

"I took pity on you. Next time I won't be so nice."

We had a very pleasant time and a very good meal. I could only handle half a plate of chicken, but Derek managed to put away the whole thing. Afterward, I suggested an ice cream cone and a walk in Schiller Park. The threat of rain had passed, and the evening was delightful. The sky was a brilliant blue with a few puffy white clouds to add interest, the breeze warm and gentle. There were walkers everywhere: some with dogs, some with baby strollers, some just walking hand in hand with loved ones, and some alone. I suggested we stop at Dream Cream, an ice cream parlor just a block from the Old Mohawk, run by my friends, Bruce and Mary. I opted for a hot fudge milkshake, and Derek chose a butter pecan cone.

"Do you feel like talking about the murder? I hate to ruin the evening, but I've been worried about you all day."

We found an empty bench at the park by the fountain with the statue of the Umbrella Girl. I told him everything, up to and including Detective Sterling's interview. The one thing I failed to mention was my commitment to investigate the murder.

"Geez, Penny, that must have been awful for you. I can't begin to imagine how Lannie must feel. I wish I could help out in some way. This whole thing is just so bizarre. I think I saw Charley Walker at the dance, if he's the one I'm thinking of. He was wearing a sport coat that was a little too snug, and he was with Stella Morgan."

"That was probably Charley."

"He also had too much to drink."

I whipped my head around to look at Derek.

"I saw the bartender refuse to serve him any more alcohol, and Stella had to lead him from the ballroom out the front door. I don't know what happened after that because I saw the other shop owners, and we started to talk. I didn't pay any attention after that."

I thought about this and asked, "Was he loud or obnoxious or causing a scene?"

"Not really. I don't think anyone else even noticed. I had just gotten a drink for myself and was leaving to find you."

We sat in companionable silence for a few moments, thinking about the dance and the fact that the very next day life had become so topsy-turvy. Derek broke the silence.

"What are you thinking about?"

"Oh, nothing really. Just that life is funny. Charley has been gone for years, and when he does come back to town, he gets murdered. I just don't understand it. It's kind of like a game of volleyball...if you don't pay attention, you get smashed in the face."

"Do you really feel like that?"

"No, not really," I admitted. "If you had asked me at any other time, I would have given a much more optimistic answer. I've actually thought about this, and I guess that, to me, life is like a tree."

"Go on." Derek seemed genuinely interested.

"Well, it's fun to climb the tree and explore each and every branch, knowing that there is a safety net to catch me if I fall. That safety net is my family and friends. I know that I can go out as far as I want on any branch, and that I'll be safe. Sometimes the climb gets tedious, and I want to rest awhile, but then I'm ready to go again. Each branch has something different to offer, so I like to spend some time enjoying it. While I'm resting, I'm serving as a safety net for others. Then I'm ready to climb even higher, exploring new things. How about you? How do you see life?"

Derek thought for a few moments and answered, "I see my life as the second half of a basketball game."

"You've hooked me, Derek. I can't wait to hear the rest of this."

"It's like this. I've played really hard the first half, just focusing on the game and not paying attention to much else. Don't get me wrong. I'm in the game because I want to be, and it is fun at some level. It's not that I think my life is half over or anything — I'm only thirty three — but I've already gotten the hard part out of the way.

"Then comes half-time and I realize that my team is ahead 50-0; there is no way to lose. I beg the coach to let me continue to play just for the sheer exhilaration of playing. I can be creative and try new things because I know I'm going to win. The moral of my philosophy is that life is fun if you eliminate the fear of failure."

This made a lot of sense to me. Derek reminded me of my mother, and my goal is to try the things I want to and not be afraid of making a fool of myself.

"I like that, Derek. I really like that." I gave him my biggest smile. "How can we be so young and yet so wise?"

"Beats me."

"Grandma Mitchell always says that wisdom comes from perspective, and perspective comes from experience. That means we both must be very experienced." Arrgh! Why do I say these things? Derek, being the gentleman that he is, decided to let that one pass.

"Come on, Penny, I'll walk you home. I know Lannie is coming over, and I've got some stuff to do to get ready for tomorrow."

"Oh, Derek, I'm so sorry! I went on and on about myself, and I did want to wish you well for your opening tomorrow. Who is going to be helping you out?"

"I hired a store manager about a month ago who is going to help with the early morning crowd. I've actually known Mike since college, and I trust him implicitly. I also hired a guy named Nick to do the baking, and he starts really early, about four in the morning. We open at seven and close at four. I don't plan on being at the shop that early, at least on most days. I think that Mike and I can rotate the early hours, giving us both some flexibility. Taylor and Thomas are going to be a big help. I have them scheduled to work from nine to three every weekday during the summer, and they say that fits with their schedules. I also have a couple of college kids who are interested in part-time work. We will have to make adjustments as problems arise, but I'm really optimistic about this venture."

"I know you'll be a big success, and your business can only be a help to my shop." I slowed down as we approached my house. "I live right here. See Tatters in the window? He loves to perch on the back of the couch and watch the world go by. He's known as the neighborhood busybody."

Derek looked at the house and said, "It's really lovely, Penny. I love old houses, and would like a tour sometime when you're not busy."

"You bet. It has all sorts of nooks and crannies. I sometimes wish I were a kid again and could play hide-and-go-seek. Tatters isn't much fun to play with because he always wins."

Derek laughed and gave me a short, friendly kiss good-bye. I could feel the promise in that kiss, and looked forward to seeing him again. I gave a small sigh of contentment as I watched him go down the street, then I turned to go into the house and use my time wisely before Lannie came over for the movie.

Chapter 8

The power of the storm was diminishing, and he could feel his own power lessening. To console himself, he thought of the three victims locked in the cellar, one with the life slowly oozing out of him, the other two ready for the treats he had in store for them. A maniacal smile appeared on his face as he planned the evening's activities...

Tatters started to bark, announcing Lannie's arrival. I wandered out to the foyer as she let herself in the front door, got down on her hands and knees to greet Tatters, and handed me a sack with the Fudge Haus logo. "We can't watch the movie without fudge to go with our popcorn. Tim just made a fresh batch and I couldn't resist."

Tim runs the Fudge Haus, just a few doors down from my house, and he is shameless. He opens the shop door while he is working the newly-cooked fudge on a large marble slab situated in the middle of the store, and the people walking by are drawn inside by the incredible smell of chocolate.

"Thanks, Lannie, this smells scrumptious." I opened the little plastic box and tasted it. "Oh, this is sooo good. You got half penuche and half chocolate mocha. I've got the movie ready to go, and the popcorn is in the micro-wave ready for me to push the button. What do you want to drink? I've got root beer, orange soda, beer, wine, or iced tea. They all go well with popcorn and fudge."

"Wow. Hard choice, Penelope. I think I'll have the beer to start with. Will you join me?"

"Of course. It's not wise to drink alone. Why don't you stick the DVD in the player while I bring in the necessities? Don't let Tatters sit in my spot."

It just doesn't get any better than this. We were having a fudge-popcorn-beer-movie fest with our favorite all-time movie. We had just gotten to the part where Bill Murray's character was driving down the railroad tracks with his two new, slightly drunk friends, when Tatters jumped off the couch and ran to the front door.

"Don't stop the movie, Lannie. I'll be back in a flash. It's probably just somebody walking by."

Tatters has very good ears. He can hear the front gate open, and warns me before my visitors get to the door. I peeked out through the leaded glass and saw a tall, smartly-dressed gentleman climb the steps and put his finger to the doorbell. I opened the door to greet my visitor.

"Good evening, Detective Sterling. Come on in. You've met Tatters." Tatters rolled over for a belly rub, and Detective Sterling could not resist. "Tatters, stop playing your cheap psychological tricks on Detective Sterling. Lannie's here and we're watching a movie." I thought for a moment and added, "You probably already knew that, right?"

Instead of answering, he headed toward the den, where we could hear Lannie laughing out loud. Poor Phil Connors was waking up once again to that haunting tune of Sonny and Cher's, "I Got You, Babe."

"Who was at the door, Penelope?" Lannie turned, saw both of us in the doorway, and muttered something under her breath. I didn't want this unscheduled visit to ruin our evening, and I didn't want Lannie and Detective Sterling at each other's throats again.

"I guess Detective Sterling has some more questions for us." I begged Lannie with my eyes to behave herself and invited the policeman into the den. I picked up the remote, pressed the "stop" button, and settled back on the couch, within poking distance of Lannie.

"Please have a seat, Detective Sterling." I gestured toward a chair facing the couch.

Instead of sitting down, he wandered over to the shelf where all my DVDs are displayed. "You have some of my favorites here: *African Queen, The Color Purple, Miracle on 34th Street… The Best of Lassie*?"

I explained that Tatters loved that movie, and he nodded as if he understood. Detective Sterling looked at the half-eaten bowl of popcorn on the table and the empty fudge container.

"Don't tell me I missed out on fudge from the Fudge Haus. I hope it wasn't chocolate mocha."

Lannie laughed. "Well, at least it gave its life for a good cause. We had it all eaten in about two minutes flat, but there is some popcorn left. Help yourself."

"No thanks." Detective Sterling sat down in the chair and absently picked up a handful of popcorn anyway. "There are a couple of things I want to clarify about Charley Walker and the time he spent in Columbus while you were married. Were you aware that he was involved in anything…um…illegal?"

Neither Lannie nor I could hide our surprise at the question, and we both looked at Detective Sterling and repeated, "Illegal?"

"Yes, illegal."

Lannie considered the question and slowly shook her head. "No, but he didn't hang out with very nice people. They weren't criminals or anything, at least I didn't think they were, but he never brought any of his friends home with him. Charley's excuse was that his friends were a little rough around the edges. They would meet at a bar for a few drinks, maybe shoot some pool, but I never really knew who his friends were. He would refer to them only by their first names. I never met them." Lannie leaned forward in her chair and scooped up the last of the popcorn. "What did Charley do to make you ask that question?"

"We put Charley's name in the national database, NCIC, and found out that he was very well known to the DPD." Before we could even start in on him, Detective Sterling made a time-out gesture with his hands and said, "That would be the Dayton Police Department."

Lannie and I just looked at each other, not knowing what to make of this information.

"Let's go make some more popcorn," I suggested, "and you can fill us in."

We all went to the kitchen. I stood in front of the microwave and decided to melt a stick of butter to put on our extra-butter popcorn.

"Penny's little brother has a theory that you can tell a lot about a person by the way he or she operates the microwave," offered Lannie.

Detective Sterling raised his brows and said, "Please continue. This sounds interesting."

I picked up the ball and said, "Thomas says that the go-getter, reckless-type people always nuke the food full power. The more cautious and deliberate people press half power, check the food, and finish cooking. The really timid ones cook on the lower levels and check the food often. Where do you fall, Detective Sterling?"

He considered for a moment and answered, "I guess I'm one of the half-power people." He looked at Lannie and said, "I bet you are full power all the way."

I stuck the butter in the microwave and started to punch the low-power button, then threw caution to the winds and jabbed one minute at full power. So there. I decided to let my wild side take over. I replenished our drinks while the butter melted, and then put the popcorn bag in the microwave.

"Oh, excuse me a minute, there's the phone." I exited the kitchen, leaving the two of them to watch the ballooning popcorn bag, and went to the den to answer the phone.

I knew even before I picked up the receiver that it was Mom checking up on me. Maybe some of her intuitiveness was finally rubbing off. I listened for a minute and responded, "Sí, Mamacita, todo está bien. Sí, sí, adiós."

I went back to the kitchen just as the microwave was dinging. Detective Sterling looked at me and said, "I heard you speaking Spanish."

"No mystery there, detective. That was my mom, and she speaks Spanish."

"I didn't know you were Hispanic."

"I'm not. I'm Irish. It's a long story, but suffice it to say that Mom is learning Spanish, and the rest of us are learning it along with her, I guess. When she starts something, she jumps in with both feet. I would say she's a full power sort of person."

I took the popcorn and put it in a big bowl, drenched it with the melted butter, and we all headed back to the den. I told Lannie that Mom had wanted to tell me that she found the final act for the talent show. The look she gave me said, "Oh, oh." I fully agreed.

Lannie grabbed a handful of popcorn and asked Detective Sterling, "What did you mean when you said Charley was in trouble with the police? I really never thought of him as a stellar citizen, but I wasn't aware of any nefarious activities."

Detective Sterling smiled at Lannie. "It's obvious you're an English teacher." He thought for a moment and continued. "It seems Charley was suspected of trafficking in the local drug trade."

"Drug trafficking? Geez, that's pretty heavy stuff." Lannie looked at me and shook her head. "I guess I'm surprised that Charley was in such deep trouble. His mother would have been destroyed."

"It seems that he was a middle man. He would buy drugs from the big shots and then sell them to the dealers on the street. The money he got from the street sellers went to pay his suppliers, and he kept a nice little profit for himself. One theory about his death is that he was ripped off by one of the street guys and couldn't pay the money owed to his suppliers. The suppliers retaliated in their own special way. It happens all the time, and the results are almost always fatal."

It was pretty obvious to us now that the drug trafficking was financing Charley's lavish lifestyle. Charley
always did have expensive tastes and liked to show off
around other people.

Lannie studied Detective Sterling's face and said,
"But you don't think that's what really happened, do
you?"

"No, I really don't think so."

"Care to tell us why?"

I could tell that Detective Sterling was having an in-
ternal war about whether or not to tell us what was on
his mind. His face was inscrutable, but I could tell with
my budding intuition that he was about to share some
information with us.

"This crime was not consistent with the usual mode
of retaliation used by drug suppliers. They kill 'execu-
tion style' for a reason: to send a message to others who
might be tempted to double cross them. The methods
vary, but they are usually 'clean' kills, with little or no
mess. Charley's death seems like a crime of passion.
The scene was very, very messy."

I shuddered at the memory and felt nauseous. I was
beginning to regret the half pound of fudge and the bag
of popcorn in my belly, not to mention the beer.

Lannie seemed very serious as she asked, "Then you
think the murderer is someone who… knew Charley?"

Detective Sterling reached down to rub Tatters's
stomach. The little fella is as easy as they come. Tatters,
that is, not Detective Sterling.

"I guess I'd have to say yes, I really do think that the
killer knew Charley and hated him. I also think that the
murder was intentional. There doesn't seem to be anything

missing from Charley's apartment. According to the autopsy, the murder took place between ten o'clock and noon, when you found the body, and the weapon was a medium-sized blunt instrument, perhaps a hammer, wrench, trophy, or even a lamp base. A larger object, a baseball bat or a shovel, for example, would have produced a different kind of wound. Nothing in Charley's apartment was the murder weapon, and everything seems accounted for, according to the condo manager."

I shrugged and looked at Lannie, who was as perplexed as I was. We really wanted to help, but didn't know how.

Detective Sterling added, "We are canvassing the entire area for the murder weapon and going door to door in the condo building trying to find some leads. I really think that we'll find that someone with an old grudge against Charley is the one who killed him. That's why I need your help, Ms. Daugherty."

Lannie furrowed her brow, deep in thought. "I will think about it, but nothing is coming to me now."

"Well, both of you, please get in touch with me if you think of anything. You have my number."

Lannie and I got up to escort Detective Sterling out. As I was opening the door for him, I noticed Tony Delamar driving away in Ms. Borden's car, an old Buick polished to perfection.

"For my money, Detective Sterling, the butler did it." He looked at me with his piercing gray eyes, and I suddenly remembered the conversation between Tony and Charley that I heard at the dance.

Detective Sterling noticed the change in my face and asked, "What is it?"

"I just remembered that I sort of…overheard a conversation between Tony Delamar and Charley at the dance. Tony, the one who just drove off, is the butler/chauffeur for Amelia Borden, who lives right across the street." I indicated which house by inclining my head.

"Does he live with Ms. Borden?"

"Not in the house. He lives in the carriage house at the back of her property."

Detective Sterling seemed very, very interested. "What were they talking about?"

"I couldn't really hear very well, but they both seemed somewhat agitated. And they acted as if they knew each other."

"What gave you that impression?"

"I really don't know." I thought for a moment, trying to remember what I heard. "I guess maybe because they were arguing about something, and you don't argue with a person who is a complete stranger."

Detective Sterling looked at Lannie and me and asked, "Do you know Tony Delamar well?"

We both shook our heads and Lannie said, "No, we don't know him at all. I told Penny he would be a great villain for her book."

Detective Sterling looked at me with surprise. "You're writing a book?"

I nodded. "It's a murder mystery. Maybe I could pick your brain sometime? I could really use your expertise."

He seemed impressed. "Sure, call me any time with any questions you may have. I'd be glad to help."

Detective Sterling and Lannie both left at the same time because it was getting late and I had to work in the morning. He offered to drive Lannie the four blocks to her house since it was dark outside. They drove off, and I thought to myself that they made a handsome couple, and hoped they didn't hurt each during the short drive.

As I was locking up and getting ready to turn in for the night, I thought about Emile's argument with Charley and made a mental note to tell Detective Sterling about it in the morning. Maybe I would pay a visit to Emile before calling the police station. Come to think of it, it was high time I made a social call to Amelia Borden, too. I could surreptitiously pump her for information about Tony Delamar. Maybe I could solve this case and write a book about it. Get ready world! Here comes Penny Mitchell, girl detective.

Chapter 9

Kevin could hear a soft moaning sound, almost inaudible because of his own harsh breathing. Moving toward the sound, he reached out with his fingers and touched a face. Kevin moved his hand to the neck and discovered a faint, thready pulse.

"Miranda, there is someone here, and he's still alive!" Kevin whispered to the injured person, "Who are you? What's wrong? How can I help you?"

Miranda followed Kevin's voice and made her way through the dark and dank prison to where Kevin was kneeling over their fellow captive. She surprised Kevin by softly and calmly saying to the injured man, "Don't worry. We're here now, and we are going to help you." But she was speaking to a dead man.

Miranda broke off suddenly as they both heard a horrible scraping sound, metal against metal; perhaps an old metal bolt, rusty from age, being dislodged from its usual place...

"Come on, Tatters, hurry up, or we'll be late for work." Tatters isn't very perky early in the morning. His frisk factor increases as the day gets longer. Come to think of it, so does mine. I was trying to hurry him along so we could get ready for work.

I wanted to get to Whimsies a little early this morning to work on the books before we had to get ready for the customers. I planned on taking an early break to head over to Full of Beans to wish Derek and the twins good luck on their first day. I was also hoping to squeeze in a quick visit to Angles to try to interview Emile about his conversation with Charley. That one would take some finesse, especially since Emile intimidated the heck out of me.

Finally, we were on our way. I like to give Tatters plenty of time to enjoy the scenery on our way to work. He'll stop to watch a butterfly flit by or, if the wind is blowing, he sticks his little nose in the air and sniffs away. What's really cute is when he cocks his head to listen to the birds chirping, almost as if he understands what they are saying. Sometimes it takes us a little longer to reach Whimsies than the five minutes I allow for walking. Tatters wags his tail and I wag my tongue along the way. One of the things I love most about the Village is being able to talk to my neighbors, who are out and about on a regular basis. I never feel lonely or isolated. There is always someone who is interested to hear about my day or share some news about a common acquaintance.

I was just about to unlock the door to Whimsies when I saw some movement through the window at Full of Beans. What the heck? I decided to take Tatters over for a little visit with Loretta. And maybe I could say a quick "hello" to Derek before he got too busy. The shop was supposed to open at seven o'clock on most days, but today it wouldn't open until eight-thirty because of the grand opening.

I tapped on the door, and Max let me in.

"Hi, Max, is Derek around?"

"Nope."

"Okay, I'll stop back later." He was probably taking Loretta for an early morning walk while Max did a last-minute check on all the equipment.

"Oh, by the way, could you stop by sometime and check the shelving in the front display case? It doesn't seem stable."

"Yep."

"And the sink in the storeroom? It's leaking."

"Nope."

"Nope?"

"Got no wrench."

"Oh. I think I may have one you can borrow."

"'kay."

"See you later, Max. And thanks."

Walking back to my store, I was musing that Tatters's vocabulary was probably larger than Max's. As Janie once said of him, "Max isn't the sharpest marble in the deck." Then I stopped dead in my tracks. What did Max mean by "got no wrench?" I knew he had one with him when he did some work for me last week. It must be a coincidence that the murder weapon was a medium-sized blunt instrument…*like a wrench*! Max was all over the Village in the course of any given day, doing odd jobs for everyone. It would be so easy to lift a tool without anyone being the wiser. This would lend credence to Detective Sterling's theory that this murder was premeditated and committed by someone who knew Charley, probably a resident of the Village.

This was one more item I put on my mental list of things to tell Detective Sterling. Maybe I should also keep my eyes open for the missing wrench, although why would the murderer bring it back to the Village? So it wouldn't be found near the murder scene? To throw suspicion on one of us? This gave me a lot to think about.

I called Lannie at a decent hour to ask for her help with a little "project" of mine. She told me she was busy until seven o'clock that night with her volunteer duty. Lannie spends several hours a week during the summer offering her services as a reading tutor for the Ohio Literacy Council. Reading has always been a passion of mine, and has given me countless hours of pleasure. I can literally spend days at the Book Loft on Third Street, browsing through the thousands of books. It amazes me that there are so many adults in our community who can't read at all. I applaud Lannie's efforts to make a difference.

Lannie and I made a date to meet at the shop at seven-thirty. I told her to wear her oldest, darkest clothes. Wednesday is garbage day in the Village, and I wanted to have a look at all the suspects' garbage before the truck came in the morning. It's not illegal to go through someone's garbage, but it would be illegal to break into a house. So we would go the legal route. Lannie would definitely not like my idea, but it's possible that we might find something to help solve the murder. I figure that anyone who knew Charley is a suspect, except for Lannie, me, Tatters, and my family.

It would be a long day for me, but Alice would be here all day tomorrow to help me. I don't know what I'll do when she retires. My sister-in-law, Grace, has been making noises about going back to work part time since Lily is no longer an infant. Grace has impeccable taste and a great business sense. I'm toying with the idea of asking her to buy into Whimsies and be my new partner.

I glanced out the window and saw some customers going into Full of Beans. It was close to nine, a little after the rush time, so I thought I'd go over to see how the twins were doing. And Derek, of course. Tatters looked at me hopefully.

"Woof, woof."

"No, Tatters, not this time. I promise to take you over to see Loretta very soon."

Tatters looked at me with those big brown eyes as if to say, "You're ripping my heart out!"

I held firm and promised him a treat. Food always makes him happy.

I trotted across the street to Full of Beans, opened the door, and went in. Taylor and Thomas were busy behind the counter, looking very cute in their denim hats and Full of Beans T-shirts. My eyes glistened with tears of pride because my baby brother and sister were now members of the working force.

"Welcome to Full of Beans. May I help you?" Thomas was so professional! He even smiled at me, the kind of bland smile you give to strangers.

"Yes. I believe I'll have a cup of the house blend...and a cheese Danish, please."

"Sure, ma'am. We'll only be a minute. Please step over to the register to pay." Thomas handed me a ticket with my order printed on it to take to the register.

"Hello," said Taylor. "Your total is four-fifty."

"Wow," I thought, "that's a decent price."

I gave Taylor a five-dollar bill, and she gave me the correct change. My baby sister is a math genius.

"Thank you so much, ma'am. Enjoy your food and have a good day."

Full of sisterly pride, I took my purchase to a table near the window and settled down to enjoy it. I saw

Derek come out of the back room, so I gave a little wave to attract his attention.

I was rewarded with a huge smile, not the bland kind you give to strangers, but the real, how-great-to-see-you kind.

"Penny, I'm so glad to see you!"

"Same here, Derek. I wanted to come over and wish you luck and see how Taylor and Thomas were doing. I'm so proud of them. They are very professional. You did a great job training them."

"They're eager learners, Penny. I've been watching them, and I couldn't be happier with the job they're doing." He looked at me and asked, "How are you doing...really?"

"I'm doing just fine... really. Lannie and I have been spending some time together talking about the murder. It's only been two days, but it seems like a month since it happened."

"I'm glad you're doing okay. I think about you a lot."

Be still my heart. Derek was looking at me with those big green eyes; I was oblivious to everything but him.

"Penny?"

"Hmm?"

"Do you want to have dinner together tonight?"

"Oh, yeah." Then I remembered my date with Lannie at seven-thirty.

"Oh, geez, I forgot. I made plans with Lannie for tonight. I'm working late, and she's meeting me at the store. Could I have a raincheck?"

"You can count on it."

"Maybe we can go to P.J.'s restaurant tomorrow. Do you like pot roast?"

"I love pot roast."

"Great! I'll get back to you later, and we'll make plans then. I had better get back to Whimsies now, but I wanted to stop in and see how things are going. I can't believe how smooth an operation this is, especially for a first day."

"Thanks, Penny. Please stop by any time." Derek stood up to escort me to the door. I gave a little wave to Taylor and Thomas, but they were busy helping customers.

I turned back and said, "Oh, another thing, Derek."

"Yes?"

"The Village Talent Show is Thursday. Would you like to go?"

"Love to. Let's talk about it tomorrow night."

I crossed the street, started to open the door to Whimsies, and then hesitated. Maybe now would be a good time to interview Emile. It was only nine-twenty; Angles didn't open until ten. I knew that Emile arrived early most days to take care of the paperwork. I would have girded my loins had I known how to do that; instead, I took a deep breath and repeated my mantra: "Sticks and stones may break my bones..."

I peered through the front window, but didn't see anyone. I considered going around to the back door in the alley but decided to knock on the window. I gave a tiny tap-tap with my fingernail. Hmm, nobody here, so I'll just go back to the store.

As I was hot-footing it back to Whimsies, the door behind me opened, and I heard a male voice say, "Whaddya want?"

"Oh, hello, Emile. How are you?"

His response was a glare.

"I guess I just, that is, er, do you have one tiny little minute to talk to me about something very inconsequential… in fact, so inconsequential it's hardly worth mentioning?" Oh, God! I was babbling, and not sounding one bit like a seasoned investigator. I asked myself, "What would Detective Sterling do?" Just then a feeling of calm came over me; I just knew I could do this.

Emile jabbed his thumb toward the inside of the shop and went in. My intuition told me that I was supposed to follow, which I did. He led me back to the salon area. Taking the bull by the horns, I said, "Emile, I heard you talking to Charley Walker a few days before he was murdered, and you didn't sound very happy with him." There, I did it. I had to resist the urge to find the nearest hole and crawl into it. "I know you had an argument, and I want to know what it was about." Was that me talking?

Emile looked very surprised, to say the least, and his jaw dropped. "Aw, shit! What were you doing listening in on a private conversation?"

I wasn't going to let Emile put me on the defensive. I looked him straight in the eye and said, "This murder was premeditated and the killer will probably spend the rest of his or her life in prison, or worse. I'm doing you a favor, because I came here before going to the police. Now, fess up." In the back of my mind I was wondering if "fess" was a word.

Emile took a deep breath, rubbed his hand over his mouth, and looked up at me under bushy eyebrows. "Yeah, Charley was here. You're right, we were arguing. But it wasn't about anything to do with his death. It was about something that happened a while back."

I remembered that Detective Sterling said that Charley's death was probably the result of an old grudge. I just couldn't picture Emile as the murderer, no matter how gruff his demeanor.

"Emile, I'm going to have to tell the lead investigator about what I heard. It would be so much better for you if you came clean to Detective Sterling before I tell him."

With a deep sigh Emile said, "Sit down, Penny."

He seated himself in the middle chair, and I tentatively asked, "I don't have to sit in the chair by the window, do I?"

Emile gestured to the chair on the other side of him, away from the window, and said, "Penny, you don't know how lucky you are that I'm not a murderer. You would have been ground up and used as hair dye by now."

I never thought of that. Emile had a point. Furthermore, nobody knew I was here right now. Thank you, God.

"I'll tell you what happened, Penny, but you have to promise not to put your pretty little nose into where it doesn't belong. You could get hurt... or worse." Emile gave me the brown-eyed version of Detective Sterling's gray-eyed penetrating stare.

I wisely kept my mouth shut and gave a slight nod of my head. That didn't actually mean that I was promising, only that I agreed I could get hurt.

It must have been enough for Emile. "A long time ago, when I was a young, stupid kid running with a bad crowd in Toledo, I got involved with a buddy's uncle who was a loan shark. I picked up some easy money by, well… enforcing a payment schedule for his clientele. I was good at it. For some reason I tend to intimidate people."

"Oh, really?"

"Yeah. After a while my conscience started bothering me. I went to see my rabbi, and he told me that God gave me special talents, and to use those talents to make myself happy. I told Rabbi Fishel that it was my dream to own and operate a salon, and he told me to go for it." Emile smiled a sweet, private smile. "That rabbi was right, Penny. A person can only be happy by following a dream."

"That's great, Emile, but what does all of this have to do with Charley?"

"One of my former 'associates' from Toledo met Charley in Dayton and told him all about my previous profession. Charley came to town to look me up. He wanted to blackmail me into giving him protection, being his bodyguard I guess, against what I don't know. He said that if I didn't help him, he would tell Dinah all about my former life."

I know Emile's wife, Dinah Schwartz. She is a lovely lady in every sense of the word. It is a mystery to me and to everyone else in the Village how those two ever hooked up. They've been married for as long as I can remember and have four great kids who, fortunately, take after their mother.

"What did you tell him?"

"I told him to get lost and to leave Dinah alone. Don't look at me like that, Penny. I didn't kill him to keep him quiet. Hell, Dinah knew all about my background. I told her before we got married. So why would I need to kill Charley?"

"I guess you wouldn't, Emile. But you still need to tell all of this to the police. If they find out about Charley threatening you, you could be in some very deep doo doo."

"Okay, okay. I'll call them before any clients come in."

"Just one more thing, Emile. Where were you between ten and twelve Sunday morning?"

"Let's see... I was probably working in the front yard. Yeah, I know I was because I saw my neighbors take off for brunch while I was weeding the flower garden. Why are you asking me these questions?" Just then we heard the front door opening. It must be Janie coming in for work. Awkwardly, I jumped out of my chair and tried to look as if I belonged there.

"Hi, Emile. Hi, Penny. How's tricks?"

"Hi, Janie. How are you?"

"I'm as good as the gettin'goes."

Huh?

Emile stood up, grunted at Janie, and headed back toward his office. I stood there, not knowing what to say.

"Hey, Penny, that dance on Saturday night was sure lots of fun. I partied like it was 1989."

And I was worried that Janie would think something was peculiar.

"Are you here doing research for your book?"

"Uh, yes, Janie, I am."

"Oh, good. Well, instead of having Amelia Borden getting electrocuted under the dryer...."

119

***

"No, absolutely not, Penelope! Are you friggin' crazy? That is the dumbest idea you've ever had."

My intuition was talking to me again and telling me that Lannie didn't like my idea of garbage espionage, or garbionage, as I like to call it. "I resent that, Lannie. I've had dumber ideas."

Lannie regarded me with affection and exasperation. "Yeah, I guess you have. Maybe the time when you convinced me to jump off your roof into the snow bank…"

"How was I to know there was a layer of ice over the snow? Anyway, you just sprained your ankle. You didn't break it."

"…or the time you wanted to tour the city and stupid me got on the COTA bus with you, and we got hopelessly lost. We finally got off the bus in some god-forsaken part of the city. My dad was furious about that one."

I could see that Lannie was just warming up, so I had to nip this in the bud. I cocked my head and gave her my best imitation of Tatters's "poor puppy-dog look," the one that always gets him an extra treat. It's irresistible when Tatters does it. I was anxious to see if it worked on Lannie.

"Oh, all right. I'm going on record as saying that this is a big mistake, and I get to say 'I told you so' when the you know what hits the fan. I don't know why I let you talk me into these things. I'm a reasonably intelligent person."

"Thank you, thank you, thank you. I was going to do this with or without you, but I'll sure feel better with you along."

"I know, Penelope, and that's why I'm going with you — to do damage control. Where do we start?"

We brainstormed a bit about the people in the Village who had contact with Charley or knew him from long ago, and came up with a list, including: Tony Delamar, Stella Morgan, Emile Schwartz (although he was way down on the list after my interview with him), Amelia Borden, Paula and Andy, Max, the handy-man, and my partner, Alice Dixon. I couldn't really envision any of these people, with the exception of Tony Delamar, being involved in any criminal activity, let alone murder. But fair is fair, and everyone was a suspect until we ruled them out. We waited until it got dark to start out on our adventure.

We decided to do this geographically. We would start with Amelia Borden's place, since her residence is the farthest south, then move towards the north end of the Village where Alice lives. Because Tony Delamar shares a garbage can with Amelia, we could knock off two at once. Lannie and I dropped Tatters off at home and, under the cover of darkness and armed with rubber gloves, flashlights, and doctors' masks, — hey, this is garbage we're dealing with — Lannie and I began the tedious task of looking through garbage cans. I had the foresight to bring along a laundry basket to transfer the contents of the garbage cans to the basket, then back to the can. We learned that Amelia received the Victoria's Secret catalogue — it was hard to imagine her in a lace teddy and a push-up bra — and that Tony had a penchant for pizza and girlie magazines. I guess I was disappointed that we didn't find a "smoking wrench" in his trash.

"Okay, Einstein, let's go to Stella's. She's next on the list, and maybe we can find out some dirt about her." Lannie actually had a twinkle in her eye. I could tell she was looking forward to this; maybe she would find something to use against Stella.

"Lannie, this is strictly confidential. We can't let anyone know we're doing this. Anyone. Ever."

"I was just funnin' with ya. As much as I would like to torment Stella, I realize that admitting I went through her garbage is going too far."

We got to Stella's and worked in silence, Lannie handing me armloads of garbage while I sorted through it and transferred the checked garbage to the laundry basket. The can was filled with empty shoe boxes, gossip magazines, bottles of hair bleach, and about a dozen empty wine bottles. After a few minutes I heard Lannie say, "Holy shit!" I was on the verge of reprimanding her for her language when she whispered, "I think I found something important."

Lannie was peering into the garbage can, her flashlight clipped to the edge. I inched over to the garbage can, peered in, and said, "Holy shit!" I looked at Lannie and her eyes were as big as saucers. "Lannie, does that look like a wrench to you?" It was lying on a section of newspaper and seemed to be stuck to it, a brownish substance on the head of the wrench and the attached newspaper.

"Uh huh."

"Now what do we do?" Just then my cell phone rang. I looked at the display. "Lannie, it's Mom. I have to take this call."

I turned my back to the garbage can to shield it from Mom while I talked on the phone. I was taking no chances. I made an effort to sound as normal as possible.

"Hi, Mom. I thought you had knitting club tonight." My mom and a group of her friends, who call themselves the "knitwits," get together every Tuesday night for a few hours and knit baby items, which they donate to Children's Hospital. "No, really, Mom, everything is just fine. Lannie and I are at Stella's house. We are just, um, getting to know her better. I'll call you if anything happens. Love you too. Bye."

I took a deep breath and tried to regroup. I shudder to think what my life would be like if I didn't have two brothers and a sister, and Mom's attention was focused solely on me. Saints preserve us!

"Lannie, Mom is really upset; she's speaking English. She knows we are up to something."

Lannie was sitting on the curb by the garbage can with her head in her hands. "Penelope, we have to call Detective Sterling; we don't have a choice. I can't wait to hear how you explain this one."

I gave her a dirty look and sent up a little prayer for inspiration. I dialed the police station and asked to be connected to Jack Sterling, hoping that maybe he was out of the office on an important case or something. No such luck.

"Um, good evening, Detective Sterling, this is Penny Mitchell. It seems that Lannie, you know my friend, Lannie Daugh..., yes, well, it seems we might have some information for you. Ha, ha. This is hard to believe, but I think we may have found the murder weapon in the Charley Walker case."

Mr. 'just the facts, ma'am' was shooting questions at me, and I felt my self-confidence disappearing. Lannie saw the look on my face and grabbed the phone.

"This is Lannie Daugherty. We are in the alley behind Stella Morgan's house on Third Street, and we found a bloody wrench in her garbage. No, I don't know the house number. Okay….okay… we'll wait here until you come." She handed me my phone and told me that Detective Sterling was going to send some uniforms to secure the area. He would be arriving shortly.

"I'm afraid the only uniforms we are going to get are the ones that have **Property of Franklin County Jail** stamped across the back in big, bold letters."

We both thought that this was funny and started laughing out loud.

"Oh, Penelope, what's wrong with us? How can we even think of laughing at a time like this?"

"Beats me, Lannie."

We found a clean spot on the pavement, plunked ourselves down, and sat for a few moments, just staring at nothing. "Lannie, does this remind you of sitting outside of Sister Perpetua's classroom waiting to get yelled at?"

"Which time? We were out in the hall fairly often as I recall. Sister said we were 'bold snips' and would end up in jail. You know, she may have been right."

Sister Perpetua is the last of a dying breed. She still teaches English and Latin at Holy Cross High School, and continues to strike terror in the hearts of young Catholic girls. Most of our teachers were lay people, and the few nuns we did have wore "street clothes," which was really funny because you could pick them out a mile away by their dark skirts, white blouses buttoned to the top, navy blazers, and sensible shoes. They also wore discreet gold crosses on a slender chain that shouted, loud and clear, I am a nun!

Sister Perpetua wore the full garb of a bona fide nun, complete with habit, wimple, rosary beads and, of course, a ruler. I used to think that novices received this preferred instrument of torture when they became full-fledged nuns. Sister Perpetua was always armed and dangerous. She definitely left her mark on us, both literally and figuratively.

Lannie smiled and said, "I remember one time she asked you to name the most famous book written by James Fenimore Cooper, and you raised your hand and answered, 'The Last of the Dominicans.' I thought it was hilarious, but I also thought you had a death wish. I bet your knuckles still hurt from that one."

I winced. That *did* hurt, but it was worth it. "I may have had a death wish, but you almost got us killed *and* sent to hell the time we were supposed to be filling the holy water fonts in all the classrooms, and you decided that if we drank some of the holy water it would make us holy and therefore impervious to the influence of the demons that made us do bad things."

"How was I supposed to know that Perpetua would be coming around the corner just as you were tipping the bottle?"

We were silent for a few moments. Finally, Lannie said, "You know why we're talking about all this stuff, Penelope, don't you?"

"Yeah, so we don't have to deal with the here and now," I sighed. "Do you think Stella really murdered Charley?"

"Nah, she's more likely to be a murderee than a murderer."

"You're probably right... although it is kind of funny to think of her getting strip-searched. Can you imagine her face when the prison matron snaps on those little rubber gloves?"

We both started laughing again.

"Do you think they accessorize prison drab with hats and stiletto heels?"

By this time we were both out of control and, wouldn't you know, Detective Sterling and the "uniforms" chose that moment to arrive.

"Do you two ever take anything seriously?"

"Well, sure…"

"Sometimes…"

"That was a rhetorical question, ladies. Now show me where you found the wrench, and tell me why you're here in the first place."

Lannie and I looked at each other, and I know we both had the same thought. It was going to be another long night.

"Hey, Penelope," whispered Lannie.

"What?"

"I told you so!"

Chapter 10

Kevin and Miranda remained as still as mice. The rasping sound must indicate that the door out of this prison was being opened. They both had the same thought: "Can we overpower this unknown captor and get out of here?" Kevin groped for Amanda's hand and tried to convey his intentions, without words, to move toward the sound and try to ...

I was standing at the counter in Whimsies having a staring contest with Whoosier, the ceramic owl Alice purchased from an estate sale in Indiana. He is perched on the top shelf of the display cabinet, and often tempts me into a staring match, which he usually wins. It had been a very long night of questions from a very grumpy homicide detective. I was hoping that Alice would get here soon so I could hide out for a while in the back office and just try to think things through. I smiled to myself at the memory of Stella coming out to the alley last night to check on all the commotion: police radios squawking, lights flashing, all the people coming to the scene like vultures attracted to rotting bodies. God, I'm getting morbid. Stella was very indignant to find out that we had gone through her garbage. It was hard to take her seriously, though, with her face a becoming shade of chartreuse that matched her green and yellow polka-dot baby doll pajamas. With her fuzzy green slippers, she actually bore a strong resemblance to Kermit the Frog.

"What do you two thugs think you are doing here?" I cringed at the memory of Stella's outrage. Detective Sterling had to intervene and tell her to back off. It didn't help matters that Lannie stood behind Detective Sterling and started making faces at her. Boy, that really set her off. I was hoping that Detective Sterling had a stun gun, but no such luck. He just threatened to cuff her and put her in jail for the night unless she settled down. Of course, Stella denied any knowledge of the wrench, or why it would be in her garbage. She even intimated that it was planted there by "the only two people in the world who don't like me." We had to laugh at that one. There must be thousands who don't like her!

Even though it was fun to see her suffer a bit, I had to admit that I was back to square one. Stella was stupid, but not stupid enough to put the incriminating wrench in her own garbage. I shivered, thinking that we were dealing with a very clever killer. I reviewed my plan and decided that I would try to interview Amelia Borden later in the afternoon, and I needed to talk to Max about his missing wrench. Good luck to me on that one! It would probably go better if I could have a few drinks first, but since he might show up this morning to adjust my display shelves, I had better forego the drinks. Drat!

I thought that it might also be a good idea to talk to Bob, the mailman. It would be interesting to see if anyone in the Village had received any correspondence from Charley. Bob would know by the return address if Charley had written to anyone. I could use a few drinks before that interview, too. I wondered if Bob had scruples and might be reluctant to share that information. Nah.

Maybe I could talk to Paula, Andy, and Alice to pick their brains. They might know something about Charley. And don't forget Tony Delamar. My list was growing and causing my brain to overload. What I really needed was to talk this over with Tatters, but I had left him home this morning. He was being a lazybones, so I gave him a day of vacation.

"Alice Dixon, where are you?" I muttered to myself. Alice was supposed to come in early today. I could really use her help now to watch the front of the store while I went back to the office to think. Whoosier was distracting me by trying to engage me in yet another contest. The current score was 400 for Whoosier and 1 for Penny. But, who's counting?

"Oh, sorry I'm so late, Penny." Alice rushed in, out of breath, carrying a big package.

"That's okay, Alice. Nothing much is happening this morning. I'm just watching the dust motes float by. We really do need to talk to the cleaning crew. What's in the package?"

"You'll never guess what I found on clearance over at the Antique Mall! Look, an exact replica of Whoosier, except for the eyes being a little crossed."

I never figured Alice for a sadist. I tried to muster some enthusiasm. "Um, that's just great, Alice. Now we have two ceramic owls."

I caught a glimpse of Max through the front window, plodding along at his usual snail's pace. "I'll be right back, Alice. I want to grab Max and ask him when he is going to check the shelving."

"Yo, Max." I leaned out the front door and yelled to his retreating back.

He turned around and looked at me with his strangely incurious expression. The man was wearing a flannel shirt, overalls, and work boots, and the temperature was supposed to reach ninety degrees today.

"Are you going to have time in the next day or so to fix the display shelf?"

"Yep."

"And the sink in the storeroom?"

"Nope."

"What if I find a wrench for you?"

"Yep."

"Uh, Max, do you mind if I ask you a question?"

"Nope."

I find it difficult in the best of circumstances to ask people questions I have no business asking. I'm a very private person, and like to think I am pretty good about respecting the privacy of others. If it weren't so important, I'd give up this interrogation business and go back to being plain, simple, live-and-let-live Penny Mitchell.

"Do you remember the last time you saw your wrench in the tool box, or the last place you used it?"

If Max thought this a funny question, he didn't show it. He took a few minutes to mull it over. I know he was thinking because his brow was furrowed and he seemed pained.

"Whimsies, last Thursday."

Omigod, that's right! Max had removed the rusted end of a garden hose from an outside faucet. I had completely forgotten about it. It was common knowledge in the Village by Thursday that Charley Walker was back in town. This meant that someone had deliberately taken the wrench for the purpose of killing Charley.

"Max, this is important. Did you use the wrench at all on Friday, or even realize it was missing?"

"Knew it was missin'. Didn't need it."

"Max, did you see anybody at all on Thursday while you were working at the side of the store? Did anyone stop to talk to you, or did you notice anyone just hanging around your tool box?"

"Saw evr'body. Busy day. Lots stopped to ask me to fix sumpin' for 'em."

"Were you by the side faucet the entire time, or did you leave for a while?"

"Went to Zang's fer a part."

Zang's is the Village hardware store about two blocks up on Mohawk. It would have taken Max at least ten minutes to go to the store, buy the part, and then return to Whimsies. Ample time for someone to filch the wrench.

"Okay, thanks, Max. I'll see you soon. Oh, and Max?"

"Yep?"

"It might be a good idea to tell the lead detective about this. I'm sure he'll be lookin' to ask some questions later." Lord, I was even beginning to sound like Max.

"'kay."

"One more thing, Max. Where were you between ten and noon on Sunday?"

Max looked at me in that special way of his and answered, "Singin' in the church choir." Who'd a thunk it? Max, a singer!

Now what? I was pretty sure that Max's wrench was the murder weapon, but I'd have to wait for the results of the forensic tests and hope that Detective Sterling would share that information. So... I knew that the wrench was probably taken last Thursday on or near the premises of Whimsies, that it was general knowledge that Charley was in town, that someone in the Village was probably the murderer because of the easy access to the weapon and the attempt to frame Stella (unless Stella did it), and I had no idea where to go from here.

I tried not to do too much thinking for the rest of the working day. I wanted to talk to several people, Amelia Borden being the next one on my mental list. I was praying for inspiration as to what I would say to her when I went to her house. "Hello Amelia, may I come in and interrogate you? Ms. Borden, did you murder Charley Walker?"

As luck would have it, Amelia was in her front yard dead-heading some geraniums when I came home early from the shop. I walked up to her wrought-iron gate and said, "Good afternoon, Ms. Borden. Lovely day." See, I knew I would be inspired.

She glanced up from her work and said, "Oh, hello, Penny dear. It's starting to get warm out here." She looked at her watch and added, "It's almost tea time. Would you care to join me?"

"Oh, yes! That would be nice. Would you give a few minutes?" I gestured across the street toward Tatters perched on the back of the couch in the picture window, watching our every move. "I'll just run home to let Tatters out, and I'll be right back."

Five minutes later I was at her front door. Amelia's house was built in 1888 and is a beautiful, imposing Gothic Revival-style house made of red-orange brick, with wrought-iron balconies under the front windows. The front door is made of intricately-carved, highly-polished wood, with one of those little thingies in the center that serves as a doorbell. I turned the knob in the little thingy and could hear the "grrrnk, grrrnk" sound that would call someone to the door.

Tony Delamar opened the door and gave me his famous leer.

"Well, hellooo there." I'm sure he was trying to sound sexy, but all he achieved was making my skin crawl.

"Ms. Borden is expecting me for tea." I felt I had gone back a century. All I needed was my calling card and a bustle.

Tony opened the door wider and gestured for me to enter. He didn't step out of the way, so I had to suck in my breath and turn sideways to keep from brushing against him. He gave me his most insolent smile, and I felt like ripping his face off. Too bad I'm so civilized.

"She'll be with ya in a minute. Have a seat in the parlor." Tony indicated a small room right off the foyer.

I asked him, "Oh, Tony, were you home late Sunday morning?"

"Wouldn't you like to know!" He gave me a good-bye leer and headed for parts unknown.

I gracefully accepted my failure to elicit a response from him and stood for a moment to take in my surroundings. Ms. Borden's parlor reminded me of Grandma Mitchell's house. The only things missing were the pictures of Pope John XXIII and John F. Kennedy. I think I remember that Amelia Borden is Presbyterian, and I strongly suspect she is a Republican.

The room had heavy draperies in the window, an ancient, faded oriental rug, dark velveteen wall coverings, oversized Victorian furniture, and lots and lots of doilies. The color scheme was an indeterminate shade of ugly. It was the perfect ambiance for an author who writes horror stories.

I heard Amelia swish into the room, and I turned to greet her. I noticed that she had changed from her denim gardening skirt into a sleeveless flowered house dress, with the toes of her support hose visible in her white sandals. I gave her my most charming smile and said, "Thanks so much for inviting me over. I hope you don't mind that I didn't dress up."

Amelia considered my khaki capris and short-sleeved blue blouse and decided to take the high road. "Not at all, my dear. I realize that you young people have a different standard of dressing."

This is amazing. Amelia is less than ten years older than Mom, but they are centuries apart in their approach to life. I would bet my life that Amelia didn't own a pair of pink sparkly flip-flops or a T-shirt inscribed with POWER TO THE PEEPHOLE. Just then, Tony rolled in a tea cart loaded with sandwiches, tea cakes, and a lovely tea service. He bowed once to Amelia and turned to leave the room. I didn't even acknowledge his presence.

"Would you like to pour, Penny dear?"

"Love to."

Gee, I hoped I was doing this correctly. I didn't attend finishing school, and I didn't want to disgrace myself or the family name. Grandma Mitchell claims that she comes from "lace curtain Irish" back in County

Cork, so I was hoping that some deep-down instinct would take over. I guess I passed muster, because I got the tea poured and the sandwiches distributed, and I didn't burp or fart in the process.

"Ms. Borden... Amelia, may I call you Amelia?"

"No."

"Uh, okay. Miss Borden, I've heard that your house is haunted." I thought I would ease into my interrogation with a little idle chit-chat. "Is there any truth to it?"

"As a matter of fact there is. This house has been in the Collier family, which is my maiden name, since the late 1800s. Years ago, maybe 1902, or maybe a little before or a little after, I can't quite remember exactly... a little girl was killed here when she fell down the stairs while playing with the children who lived here at the time, one of whom was my grandmother."

"How awful!"

"Yes, yes it was. I remember my grandmother telling me about it when I was a little girl here for a visit. My father grew up in this house, but when he and my mother married, they moved to the university area where he was a professor of history. Every Sunday after church we would come to visit my grandmother and have Sunday dinner."

I was really interested in hearing the rest of the story, so I lifted my genuine Spode teacup to take a drink, waiting patiently for her to go on.

Her eyes held that faraway look that told me she was going back in time. My mom often gets that out-of-focus look, but that is her everyday expression. Mom says it is always better to remain a little out of focus, because that's when life's little unexpected pleasures tend to show up.

Amelia continued. "My brother Ronald and I were running up and down the stairs, and my grandmother called us to her side and told us not to run on the stairs. She then told us about the horrible accident. Grandmother said that one day she and her brothers and sisters were running up and down the stairs with their little neighbor friend...what was her name? I can't quite seem to recall...oh, yes... Miriam. Miriam tripped and fell down the first flight all the way to the foyer, breaking her neck in the process."

I shivered in horror at the thought of that terrible accident.

"My brother never did want to live in this house when it came to us after our parents' deaths. My father had never talked about seeing 'the ghost,' but my grandmother said that an apparition of a little girl would appear on the staircase from time to time, especially during the summer months, and I, personally, have seen the apparition several times."

"How long have you lived here?"

"My husband and I moved in as newlyweds when my grandmother died in 1960. We spent many happy years here until he died at a too-young age in 1990."

"Did you have any children?"

Amelia Borden gave me a regal stare. "My, my. You certainly ask a lot of questions."

I flushed from embarrassment, feeling much the same as I used to feel in the presence of Sister Perpetua. "I'm just interested is all. You have been my neighbor for these past three years, and I know very little about you."

She seemed to accept my answer and gave me a tight smile. "Pour me a little more tea, would you, dear?"

I poured her tea and decided that I might as well begin my questioning before I alienated her any more. "Ms. Borden, have you heard about the Charley Walker murder?" There, I did it. I had opened the interrogation.

"Yes, Penny dear. Frankly, I was hoping to pick your brains about the murder. That's why I invited you to tea."

"Oh." Things were not progressing the way I had envisioned. I was the one who was supposed to be in control of the situation. "Why did you want to ask me some questions?"

"I heard that you were the one who found the body."

That didn't exactly answer my question, but I thought I could come back to it later. "Yes, I did find the body, and it's not something I like to dwell on. I knew Charley through my best friend, Lannie, but it was still a shock to find him like that."

"Oh, my dear, I can imagine! You poor thing. Tell me about it." Her beady little black eyes were shining with excitement.

I blurted out the entire story while she listened to every little, grisly detail. There was absolutely no sympathy in her expression; I could imagine her using the details in her next horror book. She was practically on the edge of her seat, listening to my account of the events. I wrapped up my story and waited for a comment.

"Well, that certainly is fascinating."

"Ms. Borden, had you ever met Charley Walker?"

"As a matter of fact, he came to the house last weekend to talk to my butler. I told him to go to Mr. Delamar's residence at the back of the property."

"Do you know why he wanted to talk to your butler?"

"Penny, dear, I'm not in the habit of asking questions when it's none of my business."

Ouch. "I just thought that he might mention the purpose of his visit, especially since it's obvious that he hadn't been here before."

"Why do you say that?"

"Because if he had been here before, he would have automatically gone to the back of the property where Tony lives."

"Good point, my dear. No, he didn't mention the purpose of his visit, and I didn't ask. I don't feel I can ask Mr. Delamar, either. I repeat, it's none of my business."

"Maybe it isn't your business, but the police have a right to know who Charley Walker's last contacts were. Jack Sterling is the policeman in charge of the investigation, and I know for a fact that he wants to know about Charley's movements during the last few days of his life."

"Perhaps I'll give him a call."

"Ms. Borden, the tea was very nice, but I really have to head home now. We should do this more often, maybe my house next time." Yeah, right. I can imagine Amelia guzzling beer and eating fudge.

"That would be lovely, Penny dear. Thank you for stopping by."

"By the way, Ms. Borden, were you home last Sunday morning between ten and noon?"

I find it very difficult to be subtle during an investigation and just work this question into the conversion. I have a new appreciation for our men in blue.

"Why, Penny dear, I don't know for sure. At least part of that time, I was attending services at Glen Oak Presbyterian Church. You can't possibly suspect me of any wrongdoing!"

I gave her a bland smile and let myself out the front door, wondering anew at Amelia Borden's curiosity about the murder. Was she just interested because it happened close by? Did she know more than she was letting on and just wanted to find out how much I knew? Was she just a morbid old author looking for a new story? And why would she hire somebody like Tony Delamar, who didn't have an ounce of refinement in his total being? My head was beginning to hurt again, so I resolved to stop thinking about the murder for awhile and concentrate on my upcoming date with Derek at Bixby's-on-Broad.

Chapter 11

Miranda understood perfectly what Kevin was trying to silently convey. They really were on the same wave length. Surely this was an indication that the relationship was destined for great things. She felt a surge of affection for Kevin and tried to give his hand a little squeeze of reassurance. He squeezed back, and they started moving toward what they thought was the staircase. The rasping sound was getting louder. The door would open any second, and they wanted to be in position to ambush...

"Okay, Tatters, what should I wear tonight? It's my first official date with Derek, and I want to make his mouth water." I opened my closet door and considered my options. The black Capri pants with my powder-blue silk pullover? My beige linen slacks with my ruby-red satin blouse? No one realized how much trouble I had getting dressed every day. My life isn't easy, you know. Tatters surveyed the rack where all of my tops were hanging and raised a paw to indicate his choice: my off-white linen overshirt. Of course! I could pair this with my black Capri's and a multi-colored sash around the waist of my shirt to dress up the outfit. My black high-heeled sandals and my diamond studs would complete the outfit. The total effect would be casual elegance. I felt a momentary flash of pity for Derek — how could he resist me?

I told Tatters to go sit at the front window while I finished dressing and to let me know when Derek arrived. I heard a "woof, woof" just as I finished putting on my kiss-me red lipstick, so I rushed downstairs to greet Derek at the front door.

"Hi, Penny." He gave me an appreciative look and said, "You look absolutely gorgeous."

"Come on in, Derek. Thanks for the compliment. You look very handsome yourself." Derek was wearing beige slacks and a mint-green shirt under a navy blazer. I could see a folded-up tie peeking from the pocket of his blazer. "You'll be fine without the tie. Most people get dressed up to go to Bixby's, but I've seen just about everything there. Ready to go? P.J. said he would save a window seat for us if we got there on time."

**

"We had a wonderful evening, Tatters, and I think I really, really, really like Derek. We had so much fun stuffing ourselves with P.J.'s pot roast and trying to stump each other with crossword clues." Tatters looked skeptical. "No, really, it was fun. We also talked politics and argued sports... can you believe he is a Steelers fan, too? ... and solved all the problems of the world. The only thing we didn't talk about was the murder, for which I'm grateful. I think he knew I needed to escape that nightmare for a while. What a great guy! We made plans to go to the talent show tomorrow night, and I'm looking forward to getting to know him better. I know, I know. You'll have a chance to get to know Loretta better, too. I will tell you this much, Tatters, the apartment above his shop is beautifully decorated. 'Night, Tatters, and don't hog all the covers."

***

"Good morning, Alice. I wasn't expecting to see you until later this morning." I was busy arranging our new line of vintage purses on an old coat rack when I heard Alice's key in the door.

"I couldn't sleep, Penny, so I thought I'd come in and make myself useful."

I took a good look at Alice's face and noticed the dark circles under her eyes. She was trying hard to be cheerful, but I could tell it was an effort. I wanted to talk to her about the murder and pick her brain about a few things, but I wasn't sure about the timing. Grandma Mitchell always says that everything from food to relationships can be ruined by bad timing.

"I came in early myself. Paula and Andy were due in for the early shift, but I called them and asked them to come later. I want to leave in plenty of time to get a seat at the talent show. Are you planning to go?"

I had been fussing with the purse display while talking to Alice and not looking at her. My question went unanswered for too long, so I turned to see if she had heard me. She was still standing by the door with her key in her hand, not moving. Her brow was furrowed as if she was concentrating on something. This behavior was totally alien compared to anything I'd ever seen from Alice. Granted, she is from the generation of women who slept on brush rollers, which I'm sure caused some brain damage, but Alice is always engaged in the moment. Our customers revel in the total attention she gives them and her ability to stay focused solely on them.

"Alice…Alice, are you okay?"

She visibly roused herself, giving me a weak semblance of a smile.

"Oh, yes, Penny. I'm just fine…just thinking about what I want to do today."

I didn't believe that for a minute, but decided to let it pass. Alice is one of the most organized people I know. She plans in advance for every possible contingency, and her schedule is mapped out days in advance. Heck, I had teachers in school who laminated their lesson plans who were nowhere near Alice on the organizational scale. I headed back toward the storeroom for the broom and the watering can and told Alice I was going to sweep the front walk. The geraniums soak up the morning sun and always appreciate a little extra sip of water. The sweeping would allow me a little alone time where no one could see my thoughts. I also wanted to give Alice some time to compose herself.

Lannie walked up just as I began sweeping. "Hey, Penelope, how was the big date?" Before I could answer I heard Lannie groan. "Don't look now, but here comes Polka Dotty."

I cringed at the word "polka." I turned and saw Stella Morgan going into Full of Beans wearing a black-and-white polka dot sundress with a matching ribbon on her over-sized straw sun hat and gorgeous little sling-back stiletto heels. She looked good.

"Do you think Stella has ever had cosmetic surgery?"

"Don't know. She could sure use a personality enhancement, though."

"Well, Lannie, you have to admit that Stella can still turn heads at her age."

Lannie just shook her head and commented, "If I wore those clothes, I'd look like Raggedy Ann in Barbie clothes. Honestly, how can she walk in those shoes? Oh well, I feel just as sexy in my Birkenstocks, and I won't have those disgusting pointy little things on my feet in ten years."

"You're a real woman, Lannie, and you'd look beautiful in anything."

"Hear me roar! Spoken like a true friend, Penelope. I might consider wearing open-toed Birks to show off my new Luscious Lollipop nail polish…"

"Or high-heeled Birks to showcase those lovely ankles…"

"How about the sexy ankle-strap Birks…"

"Oh, Lannie, you are in the dictionary under 'silly.' You know," I mused, "every time I see Stella it reminds me of one of Father Brennan's sermons."

Lannie looked at me as if I had a banana sticking out of my ear. "You can't be serious, Penelope. No one ever listened to one of Father Brennan's sermons. He had the ability to lull a ferret on amphetamines into a stupor."

Lannie was right. When we were growing up we had to endure countless homilies by the man. P.J. and I used to make bets every Sunday to see who could follow his sermons for the longest amount of time. I tried, I really tried, but after a few minutes I would start thinking about what I would wear the next day, or if the lady in front of me colored her hair, everything under the sun except for holy thoughts. We would whine to our mother, and she just answered by saying that Father was brilliant and gave "esoteric" talks. P.J. and I always referred to Father Brennan as the original "esoterrorist."

"You're right, Lannie, but I remember one time when he was quoting the famous analyst, Carl Rogers. That got my attention because I was starting to become interested in psychology. Anyway, Father said that Carl Rogers thought of people as sunsets and that he wouldn't change their colors, a little more orange here or a little less purple there, because that would change the essence of the person. Each person is as unique as a sunset, and just as beautiful."

"Bull, Penelope. Stella is not a sunset; she's more of a solar eclipse."

By this time we were dissolved in giggles. Wouldn't you know that that was when Detective Sterling decided to make his appearance!

"Do you two do your grocery shopping at Piggly Giggly?"

I was shocked. That button-down exterior masked a keen sense of humor.

"Hello, Detective Sterling," we murmured in unison.

"Have you two ladies recovered from your evening of garbage snooping?"

I, at least, tried to look contrite, but Lannie forged full-steam ahead.

"Hey, if it weren't for us, you wouldn't have found the murder weapon. I would think you would get down on your knees and thank us for our help."

Detective Sterling had the audacity to smile at Lannie's indignant reply. If anything, I was encouraged that he didn't seem to be exasperated with us.

I ventured to ask a question. "Did you get a chance to have the wrench analyzed? Is it the murder weapon?"

Lannie jumped in. "Were there fingerprints? Could you tell if it was Max's wrench?"

"That's why I'm here, ladies. I thought you might be interested in the lab results. The wrench you found in Ms. Morgan's trash was, indeed, the murder weapon. The blood and hair found on the wrench were consistent with the samples we took from the body." He must have noticed that all the color had left my face, and that Lannie didn't look much better. In fact, I was in imminent danger of losing my breakfast.

Lannie said weakly, "I think... I need...to sit down."

Detective Sterling grabbed her by the arm and ushered her into the shop. I followed behind and heard him yell to a startled Alice, "Get us some hot, sweet tea."

Alice just stood there staring blankly at us.

"Tea...now!"

That galvanized her into action. I pointed to the office door, and we made it to the chairs before I immediately stood up and rushed to the bathroom. I did keep my breakfast, barely, and the cold, wet paper towels applied to my face helped me feel almost normal. I grabbed some extra towels and held them under the cold water to take back to Lannie. When I got back to the office, Lannie was sitting in her chair staring at nothing, with Detective Sterling kneeling next to her, holding her hand, and speaking to her in a soft, gentle voice. I noted this scene in the back of my mind and decided to think about it later.

"I'm okay," I said to no one in particular. Neither one paid any attention to me. "I...said... I'm... okay!" I practically shouted. This time they both looked at me and nodded. Boy, did I feel invisible! I peevishly threw the towels at Lannie.

"Here, maybe this will help."

Lannie looked at me and smiled. "Thanks, Penelope. I don't know what came over me. I guess…I guess this whole business just came crashing down on me. It's okay to think of the murder as a puzzle, but suddenly it became so…*personal*. I'm better now. Thanks."

I instantly felt contrite. I remembered that we were talking about a real person, a person Lannie had loved at one time.

Alice arrived with the tea and excused herself after asking if she could help in any way. I signaled her with my eyes that I would fill her in later. She left us to get back to her customers.

Lannie murmured, "I don't know what to say. Should I be happy that we found the murder weapon and that the investigation can go forward? Or should I just feel sad that Charley drove someone to murder? I'm kind of numb emotionally right now. It's as if I'm in a parallel universe or something."

I nodded. I knew just how Lannie felt. This whole situation was so alien compared to anything else we had ever experienced. The odd part was knowing that murders happen all the time, all over the world, affecting thousands of people every day, the same as it was affecting us.

Detective Sterling released Lannie's hand and stood up from his kneeling position to take a chair close to Lannie. He glanced at me and motioned to the chair across from them. I sat down, and we all stared at the wall for a few moments.

I finally asked, "Does this help with the investigation? I mean, knowing the wrench was the murder weapon?"

Detective Sterling answered, "It helps any time we find a new piece of evidence or hear new information." He gave a deep sigh. "Solving a crime rarely ever goes in a straight line. The clues seem to zigzag all over the place, and it's up to the police to follow the clues and make sense of them. I'll be honest with you; this is a tough case because there are a lot of people with a motive to kill Mr. Walker. That happens any time drugs are involved. Add that to the fact that that we're dealing with two cities. We can't rule out that someone from Dayton came to Columbus, either to intimidate or to kill Mr. Walker." He looked at me and smiled. "I know that Mr. Walker tried to hire someone to be his bodyguard, so he must have felt threatened."

Emile must have gone to the police station shortly after I talked to him and told Detective Sterling about the argument I overheard between him and Charley.

At that moment, there was a tippy-tap at my office door. I knew immediately to whom that tippy-tap belonged. My suspicions were confirmed when one cornflower-blue eye appeared in the crack of the door, followed by a neon-orange T-shirt with FREE MARTHA written across the front in bright yellow letters. A compact little body wearing denim shorts and orange tennis shoes entered the room and said, "¿Hay un problema?"

My Spanish must have been improving, because I was starting to understand everything Mom said.

"No, Mamacita, come on in. Have you met Detective Sterling, the lead investigator in the Charley Walker homicide?"

"No, we haven't met. Encantada, Detective Sterling." My mom dimpled him into speechlessness as she held out her hand. I don't know how she does it, but I've seen it happen a million times.

He took her hand and just stared at her. My mom is a happy little person; nothing ever gets her down. She just seems to exude goodwill toward others, and it can be overwhelming.

I decided to give the poor man a few moments to compose himself. "Detective Sterling is just catching us up on the latest developments in Charley's murder. Was there something special you wanted, Mom?"

"I wanted to remind Lannie to come over to the rec center to practice her piano piece with the twins for their magic show. They get off work today at three." My mom turned toward Detective Sterling and said, "I do hope you are planning to attend the talent show tonight. I promise you will be amazed. ¡Será fantástico!"

He seemed flustered and started stammering, "I…well…the thing is…"

Lannie interrupted, "I'm sure Detective Sterling will be too busy with his investigation, Angela."

The homicide detective snapped out of his daze at the mention of the investigation. "As a matter of fact, it probably wouldn't hurt to take a few hours off, especially if most of the people from the Village will be there. It will give me an opportunity to observe the suspects without them being aware of my presence."

Hmm, I hadn't thought of that. This would be the first time since the murder that everyone would be together in one place.

"¡Excelente!" exclaimed Mom. "I look forward to seeing you there. Penny darling, I was just at Full of Beans and Max said to tell you he would stop by momentarily to fix your shelf and look at the sink. By the way, Derek and Loretta send their best, and Derek said to tell you to save him a seat at the talent show."

I got a warm, fuzzy feeling in the region of my heart at the mention of Derek's name.

Lannie looked amused as she asked, "Hey, lover girl, do you want to have an early dinner at Barcelona tonight? I could sure go for some of their paella to get me through the talent show, especially if the magic show turns into last year's disaster."

"Thanks anyway, Lannie, but I promised Tatters he could have dinner with me here tonight since we haven't had much quality time lately. I want to work up until the show on the mountain of invoices on my desk." I glanced an apology to Detective Sterling for Lannie's rudeness. We were treating the poor man as if he were invisible.

Max stuck his head through the doorway just as Mom left. "Here to look at yer shelf and sink."

"Hello. Max. I didn't know you were here."

Max answered, "If yer not where yer at, yer nowhere."

I let that sink in while I reached behind me and grabbed my tool kit from the cupboard. Max looked in horror at the spiffy, daisy-covered toolbox I had ordered from Nieman Marcus as a present to myself when I came to work at Whimsies. Max gingerly opened the box and backed away, shaking his head.

"Can't use those tools."

"Why not?"

"Covered in daisies."

I was incensed! I couldn't believe anyone wouldn't just love my hammer, screwdriver, and wrench set with the beautiful, hand-painted, porcelain handles. They were to die for.

Detective Sterling had covered his face and odd, choking sounds were coming from his vicinity. It dawned on me that these men weren't taking my tool kit seriously.

"What's wrong with you guys? These tools cost more than a Ralph Lauren suit!" I tried to calm down and think. "Okay, Max, what if I covered the handles with duct tape? Could you use them then?"

Max considered the question and gave a quick nod. Well, quick for him anyway. I could tell he was less than thrilled, but I considered this a victory.

Lannie sneered. "Here, Penelope, hand me the tape. I'll cover the handles so Max doesn't have to contaminate his hands."

By this time, Detective Sterling had composed himself. He looked at Lannie and said, "I haven't had paella in a long time. Let's meet at Barcelona at five-thirty and that will still give you plenty of time to be at the rec center before the show starts." His demeanor was very nonchalant, but I noticed him studying Lannie intently.

She was momentarily flustered but managed, "Sounds like a plan." And that was that. Lannie finished her taping, and they both got up to leave. I watched them walk out together while thinking that this was certainly an interesting development.

I called out to Lannie's retreating back, "Hey, Lannie, in case I don't see you before the talent show, break a finger."

I envied them their dinner at the Barcelona. It is one of my favorite restaurants in the Village. It has the best outdoor dining area in Columbus. Scott, the owner, treats all of his patrons like royalty. His staff is well-trained and friendly, and Chef Paul is a master. Paul and P.J. are good friends, and often go out together after work. Chefs' hours are long and hard, and a person has to have a calling to devote so much time to food. Lucky for me.

One of the reasons I love German Village so much is that there are a variety of places to eat. Even if I decide to stay home and cook, there are two supermarkets in the Village that carry every kind of food item imaginable. A person could be born in the Village and live his or her whole life here without ever leaving because all of the amenities are within walking distance. I am literally fifteen minutes or less from work, doctor and dentist, dry cleaner, library, vet, various shops, hair salon, church...the list is endless.

Max fixed the shelf and the sink, and I was finally left alone in the office. I tried to gear myself up mentally to tackle the invoices. No luck. My brain was swimming with the list of things I would have to do to solve this murder. I decided to put it all down on paper so I could investigate in an orderly manner. I watch *Forensic Files,* and the investigators put their information on a big board to keep all the information straight. I didn't have a big board, but I did have my leftover paper bag from last week's lunch and a Sharpie pen.

- Charley was killed with Max's wrench by some-one who knew him
- the perpetrator tried to implicate Stella by putting the wrench in her trash
- the murder took place during the late morning on Sunday
- I am having a heck of a time trying to verify eve-ryone's alibi
- I still need to question Bob, Andy, Paula, Tony, and Alice
- I have no idea where to go next

I heard the jangle from the shop door and Alice greeting Bob, the mailman. Now would probably be the best time to ask Bob if Charley had written to anyone in the Village. I prayed for patience and vowed to be nice and sweet to Bob.

"Good morning, Bob." I pasted a smile on my face as I walked from the office. "How are you this fine day?" Wrong thing to say.

"Well, Penny, I have this funny rash on my shoulder that has been bothering me for two days. The doctor gave me some ointment and told me to put extra padding between my shoulder and my mail bag. Did I tell you my mother-in-law has shingles? I'm hoping you can't catch that stuff by eating the same food. She was over at our house on…"

As I was rolling my eyes in agony, I spied Whoosier from his perch high above Bob's head smirking at me.

That owl was definitely starting to annoy me. I made a mental note to myself to get the stepladder from the storeroom and turn that smug face of his against the wall.

"Sorry to hear about your troubles, Bob." I hurried on before he could get another word in edgewise. "I have one very quick question for you."

Alice was standing behind the counter sorting through the mail Bob had just handed to her, and shot me a startled glance. I'm sure she was wondering why I was engaging Bob in conversation when I generally go to great lengths to avoid the man.

"I was just wondering if you had delivered mail to anyone in the past several weeks with a return address from Charley Walker."

"Well, now, Penny, that's an interesting question. Sometimes I notice return addresses and postmarks, and sometimes I don't. Why, just the other day I delivered a letter to old Mrs. Fenner who lives on Frankfort. I noticed that it came from Nairobi, and wondered if she had friends there. People who live in the Village get mail from all over the world."

Arrgh! I grabbed his arm and turned him toward the door. I was hoping that walking would speed up his mental processes, and that I could get a straight answer from him before we did his whole route.

"But did you notice a letter from the Polson Building? Or a return address from Charley Walker?"

"I don't think so. Let me have some time to think about that, okay? Sometimes I'll remember something clear out of the blue. I guess it was about a week ago last Tuesday, or was it Wednesday?…well, anyway…"

"Bob," I interrupted, "just think about it and let me know. Better yet, just leave me a note when you deliver the mail." I was brilliant!

"I can do that, Penny."

"Thanks, Bob." I started to walk back to the shop, stopped suddenly, and turned back toward him. "Bob, I remember when you were in Whimsies the other day talking to Lannie. You said something about understanding how she was feeling because you had lost someone, too. What did you mean?"

If Bob thought I was being nosey, he didn't give any indication.

"Oh, Penny, it was so sad. About fifteen years ago I lost my favorite niece in a car crash. She was riding with some other kids, and the car went out of control and struck a light pole. Two of the kids were killed instantly. I really haven't gotten over it yet."

"I'm sorry, Bob. That sounds absolutely awful."

"It was. Alice and I never mention it. Well, gotta go. See you tomorrow."

I stared at him. "Alice? Alice Dixon, my partner?"

"Yeah. See you later, Penny." Bob gave me a salute and started on his way. The one time I want to talk to him, he decides to cut the conversation short. Go figure!

This news was very disturbing. What could the niece's death have to do with Alice? Why wouldn't they talk about it? I watched him head down the street, thinking I would catch him tomorrow and ask some more questions, although I had no idea what those questions would be. Was this something I could bring up with Alice? Why had she never mentioned the fact that she had known Bob for fifteen years or more? I turned to head

back to Whimsies and saw Janie emerge from the doorway of Angles. She must have been on her mid-morning
break, because she had a can of soda pop in her hand.

"Hey, Janie, what's up?"

"Hi, Penny. I've got a few minutes before my next
client and thought I would take advantage of the sunshine." She plopped herself down on the front stoop and
took a long swallow. "How's the book comin'?"

"I'm breezing right along," I lied. "Have you been
busy this morning?"

"Yeah, it's been nonstop for the past hour. But I like
it when it's busy because time files."

Files? Must be manicurist talk.

"We learned the expression in Latin class: 'tempus
fugit.' It means that time flies, well, literally, time
flees."

"Hmm. Well, tempus fugits faster and faster all the
time."

"Well, nice talking to you, Janie. See you later."

At least I had a smile on my face when I went back
to the shop. I can't always understand Janie, but she
makes my day a little brighter.

Alice was busy with some customers when I entered
the shop, so I went back to the office to wrestle with
those darn invoices. I hit my groove and found myself
famished after two hours of steady work. I went out to
the customer area to tell Alice that I was going home for
lunch and to get Tatters to bring back with me. She was
on the phone, so I pointed toward my house and my
stomach, and she seemed to understand. She waved me
out of the store and went back to her conversation.

Chapter 12

Kevin and Miranda were as quiet as they could be. The maniac thought they were still bound, so they had the element of surprise. They would grab him by the legs as he came down the stairs and, between the two of them, would hold him down. One thing they didn't count on was the light switch. The madman flicked the switch as soon as the door was open, and blinding light flooded the basement...

"Get your leash, Tatters. It's two o'clock already, and I have to be back at the shop. Alice is probably dying of hunger." I stuck a can of microwaveable chicken and rice soup in my purse to have for dinner. It would be perfect after gorging myself on my super-sized ham and Swiss on rye for lunch.

We enjoyed our short walk back to Whimsies, although Tatters tried to turn it into a long walk. We reached the corner of Kossuth and Fifth just as a tour bus from Pittsburgh was unloading, its passengers heading toward Schmidt's Sausage Haus for a late lunch. Tatters loves the tourists, and the tourists love him.

"Oh, what a cute puppy!" is the usual response, and the little critter eats up the compliments. He shamelessly begs for treats which, strangely enough, many of the women carry in their purses. Tatters shot me an angry glare as I hurried him past the bus. He takes his treats very seriously.

We arrived at the shop to be greeted by Paula and Andy.

"Where's Alice?" I asked, not expecting to see them there so soon.

"She called and asked if we could come in a little early, since she had errands to run before the talent show. She said we could close the shop early today because of the show." Andy held up a sign he had made to let potential customers know that Whimsies would close tonight at seven. "This way we can see the whole show."

"That's great." What else could I say? I was disappointed that I couldn't question Alice about Bob's statements but, as Mom always says, "¡Así es la vida!" I was trying to think of a way to ask them what they knew about Alice without sounding gossipy.

I unhooked Tatters's leash, and he ran to Andy for a belly rub. The fickle little guy was still mad at me for not stopping at the tour bus. My friend, Vita, from high school, would always say, "Put on your big girl panties and get over it!" I almost said that to Tatters, but thought better of it in the presence of Paula and Andy.

I tried to be as nonchalant as possible and said, "I talked to Bob today, and he said he knew Alice from way back when."

Andy was still busy tending to Tatters, so Paula answered. "We wouldn't know about that. We didn't really know Alice well until we came to work here. We've lived in the Village for six years, and Alice has been here even longer, but our paths rarely crossed."

Now what? I couldn't belabor the point, or they would become suspicious of why I was asking. I guess I would just have to wait for the right time and ask Alice about it myself.

"If you two want to unpack the latest shipment, Tatters and I will take care of the front of the shop. And, Andy, could you get me the stepladder from the storeroom?"

***

I got to the rec center, after dropping Tatters off at home, in plenty of time to find two seats together in a good location. The place was buzzing. I tilted my two chairs forward in the universal signal of "these chairs are taken!" and made my way to the refreshment table to say hello to P.J and Grace.

"Who's watching Lily tonight?" I asked, as I gave them both a kiss.

Grace answered, "She's at the Murphy's tonight and enjoying every minute of it."

P.J. and Grace are blessed with wonderful neighbors. Steve and Julia Murphy have a son, Jimmy, who is just a little younger than Lily. She loves spending time at their house and "mothering" little Jimmy. Steve and Julia were slated to do the Tango at the talent show until Steve sprained his ankle. They were not going to be able to attend, so the babysitting arrangement worked out perfectly for P.J. and Grace.

"I haven't seen my favorite niece in way too long. Why don't I stop by on Tuesday after breakfast to pick up Lily, and she can spend the whole day with me? We can go to the park in the morning and do girlie stuff the rest of the day."

Grace thought that would be a marvelous idea. That would also give me a chance to talk to Grace about coming to work at Whimsies for a few hours a week.

"The hors d'oeuvres look fabulous!" I spied several of my favorites: smoked salmon wraps, buffalo-style chicken bites, bacon wrapped shrimp and, my favorite, artichoke dip. I was glad that I had eaten a light dinner because I was determined to try everything. I grabbed a bottle of water from the end of the table and noted that Tony Delamar had just escorted Amelia Borden into the room.

"Excuse me for a moment, you two. I just saw my neighbors come in and I want to talk to them." I gave P.J. and Grace a little wave and took off toward the door.

Amelia spotted me before I reached them and gave me a tight little smile.

"Hello, Penny dear. How are you this evening?"

"Just great, Ms. Borden. And how are you two?" I included Tony in my greeting, hoping that would make it easier for me to ask him some questions later on.

Amelia just gave a polite little nod and headed toward the chairs. Tony lingered a moment and moved a little too close, whispering in my ear, "Do ya want to sit by me?"

I made a determined effort to keep my knee straight because it was just about ready to shoot right to his groin area. "Darn, Tony, I can't because I'm meeting someone." I congratulated myself for saying this with a straight face. "But I am curious about something. How long have you worked for Amelia Borden?"

"About five years. Why, Penny darlin', you really *are* interested in me."

162

I swallowed the bile that rose in my throat and forced myself to smile.

"Oh, just curious about my neighbors, that's all. Um, have you always been a butler?"

"No, before that I was an airplane mechanic at Wright Pat."

Hallelujah! Wright Patterson Air Force Base is in Dayton, Ohio. I quickly did the math and discovered that there was a two year period during which both Charley and Tony lived in Dayton. They could have known each other from there.

"That's interesting. Say, I used to have a friend who lived in Dayton. Did you ever meet Charley Walker when you lived there?"

Tony's face clouded over, and he moved even closer. "Why are you asking these dumbass questions, lady? Some people are a little too nosey for their own good." Remembering that he was in a room full of people, he backed off a little, rearranged his face into a more pleasant expression, chucked me on the chin, and started to head toward where Amelia was sitting. "See ya later, sweetcakes."

I had an undeniable urge to take a shower right then and there. This was definitely information I intended to share with Detective Sterling. I remembered that he was coming tonight, so I looked around the huge room to see if he had arrived yet.

The room was filling up quickly. The lights started to flicker, indicating that everyone should be seated. I started toward my reserved chairs and saw Derek standing at the refreshment table with P.J. and Grace. I raised my arm to catch his attention and pointed to the chairs.

He nodded and joined me just as the show was beginning.

It was a really fun two hours with no disasters this year. Emile and Dinah Schwartz entertained us with a delightful tap dance routine to "Singin' in the Rain;" the German Village Men's Choir performed a medley of show tunes; and Max stole the show with his ventriloquist act. His little dummy was dressed in work overalls and a flannel shirt. Horace, the dummy, even had a miniature tool belt around his waist. Max would ask him long and involved questions, and Horace would answer in monosyllables. It was absolutely hilarious.

Taylor and Thomas were fantastic with their magic act. The audience "oohed and aahed" all through their performance. I liked how the twins invited audience participation. They would ask someone to pick a card and would retrieve that very same card from a person in an entirely different section. I was so proud of them, and Lannie did a fine job accompanying them on the piano. The whole routine was quite dramatic, and they received a standing ovation.

Immediately before the final act, Derek stood up and excused himself. I expected him back momentarily, and was very surprised when he walked on the stage with the next group, carrying his saxophone. It was Mom's choir group! The singers were resplendent in their black robes and white satin sashes. Mom came on stage and with a one…and a two…and a three, started belting out a song. It took me a few minutes to recognize the tune as "Stagger Lee." What Mom lacked in talent, she made up for in enthusiasm. Luckily, the rest of the choir drowned her out most of the time, and when they took a breath, the sax started wailing. Every once in a while I could hear an off key word or two. "Stagger…shot…please don't…" To Mom's credit, the whole room was rocking. Everyone enjoyed the show, and I was touched and impressed by Derek's willingness to help out.

Nobody was eager to leave after the show, so we all stayed around for a while to chat and enjoy the rest of the food. Derek stayed with me the entire time. I could relax and enjoy his company without worrying about Tony. Lannie and Jack Sterling disappeared to some secluded spot, so I wasn't able to pass along my information to him about Tony living in Dayton. I guess that could wait until tomorrow.

Derek offered to walk me home after we had had a chance to visit with everyone. It was late when we got home and, since I didn't have to work the next day, I invited Derek in for a drink. He declined, saying he had to work early, but asked if Tatters and I would like to join Loretta and him for a picnic at Schiller Park at noon the next day. He said he and Loretta would supply the food. I told him I would have to check with Tatters but that I was all for it. He kissed me goodbye, and I went in to tell Tatters about the evening.

***

I knew I was late for class because the bell was ringing, and it wouldn't stop until I got to my Spanish classroom. The quicker I went, the farther away the room became. The bell wouldn't stop…someone was hitting me on the shoulder.

I slowly awoke and realized I was dreaming. Tatters was pawing me on the shoulder.

"Stop it, Tatters, I'm sleeping!"

I noticed the phone was ringing and leaned over to answer it. My bedside clock read two seventeen. I was still too sleepy to be alarmed by the ringing phone in the middle of the night.

"Hello?"

A very low voice whispered, "Your store is on fire."

I quickly came awake. "What?"

I heard a click and then the dial tone. I shook my head to get rid of the cobwebs and stared at the phone. Had I heard correctly? It sounded like someone said the store was on fire. Would the fire department call me and then hang up? I didn't wait around to figure out what was happening. It would only take me a minute to run over to Whimsies to check that everything was okay. I put on my sweats, grabbed my keys, and headed out the door.

Within two minutes I was standing at the front door of Whimsies. Everything seemed to be in order. I glanced around and, for the first time, noticed how dark it was. There was cloud cover, so there was no light from the moon. Everything was so very quiet, except for the distant rumble of thunder. I knew a big storm was on the way, and we were due for some rain. I gave a fleeting thought to Tatters, and hoped I would be home before the storm hit. He gets frightened by thunder and lightening and hides under my dining room table.

I opened the door with my key and peered into the shop. The layout of the store is similar to many in the Village, since most of the stores are converted houses.

From the doorway I could see into the front room, which is the display area. A short hallway leads to my office in the back, which used to be a kitchen, and behind that is the storeroom, which was once a bedroom. There is a basement door beside the restroom, which is situated just off the little hallway.

I entered the front room and locked the door behind me. I switched on the lights and walked a little farther into the room. I reached the hallway and noticed the basement door was wide open. We never use the basement. First of all, I'm scared to go down there because there are cobwebs and a dirt floor. There is absolutely nothing inviting about our basement — the only time that anyone goes down there is to service the furnace, the water heater, or the alarm system. It occurred to me that the alarm wasn't set because I didn't hear the annoying "beep-beep" that continues until the alarm is disarmed. This seemed very strange, because the last person out of the store at night always sets the alarm.

I moved toward the basement door and started to close it. No way was I going down to investigate, especially in the middle of the night with a storm brewing. This was a situation that could wait until the light of day when several people were around to give moral support.

As I reached toward the open door, I heard a soft *whoosh* behind me and started to turn. Then came the blinding pain at the back of my head, then nothing…

I awoke to a monster headache and a general feeling of discomfort. My face was smooshed in the dirt floor, so I tried to lift myself. I slowly became aware that my hands were tied behind my back and that my feet wouldn't move when I commanded them to. They must be tied too. This whole situation seemed eerily familiar. Omigod! I wondered if Kevin and Miranda were in the basement with me. I forced myself to calm down and try to remember what happened. This was no simple feat, since every molecule in my body hurt. I remembered the talent show, going home and falling asleep, and the phone call. The store was not on fire, so someone lured me here to inflict bodily harm. I wondered why that person didn't just kill me instead of tying me up.

I must have blacked out again, because I found myself waking up once more. My head was throbbing. I moved my face to one side, and it felt all wet, kind of a sticky wet. Could that be blood? Every time I was scared or upset as a child I would sing, "She'll Be Comin' Round the Mountain." It was my favorite song because it soothed me. I tried to open my mouth to sing a verse or two and discovered that I had a gag in my mouth. I decided to go back to my thinking so I wouldn't get hysterical. It was like that game we used to play as kids: "Whatever you do, don't think of an elephant wearing a pink bikini." Of course, it was impossible to do that. I needed to think about my situation in practical terms. I figured that the reason the person didn't kill me was because I could be down here for weeks. By the time I was found, I would be a skeleton! This wasn't helping.

"Ooh, turn off the light. It's killing my eyes!" I thought I was saying it out loud, but no sound came. I closed my eyes tightly against the glare, but my ears starting sorting out sounds. I heard a "woof, woof," and was ready to yell at Tatters for waking me up. Tatters! Tatters found me!

Gentle hands were checking for a pulse. Someone said, "Thank God, she's alive."

Someone else answered, "I knew she had a hard head."

Yet another voice from upstairs said that the squad was on the way. How many people were here anyway?

Tatters was licking my face and jumping up and down. I could hear Mom's soothing voice saying, "Don't worry, Penny darling. I'm just going to untie these bindings and get the blood circulating again. Hush...don't try to talk and stay as still as you can. I know it hurts, baby, hush."

The next time I woke up I was on my back, and could feel Mom gently massaging my arms and legs. It still hurt to open my eyes all the way, but found I could squint without too much pain.

"What happened? What time is it? Who did this? I thought the shop was on fire. How did you find me?" My voice sounded hoarse to my ears.

Lannie answered this time. Lannie was here? "I got another SOS call from your mom. Jack and I, uh, Jack hadn't gone home yet... ran over to your place and rang the bell. We could hear Tatters barking his little head off, but you never came to the door. We called Angela and she came right over. When we went in and found you gone, Jack had the bright idea" — I could hear the pride in her voice — "to put Tatters's leash on to see if he would lead us to you. That's just what this wonderful little guy did! Tatters, that is, not Jack, although he is wonderful, too."

"But how did you get into the store? I distinctly re-member locking the door."

"That's where I come into the picture." I recognized Paula's voice from somewhere off to my left. I tried to turn my head, but the stabbing pain convinced me to lie still. "Lannie called and asked me to come over with my key. Tatters was scratching at the front door and refused to budge." Goodness, I hope he didn't mar that beautiful wood. "We came in, and he ran straight to the basement door and started making those gargled little sounds in the back of his throat like he does when he's upset." Yeah, he sounds just like Chewbacca.

By this time the squad had arrived. They sounded like a herd of elephants pounding down the stairs. I wondered in a distant part of my mind if they were wearing pink bikinis. The pain in my head was unbearable, and I could feel myself starting to lose consciousness again. Before I sank into oblivion, I knew there was something very important I had to tell Detective Sterling. Oh yeah, about Tony.

I croaked in his general direction, "Detective Sterling, I think you need to talk to Tony Delamar. He lived in Dayton at the same time as Charley." If I had mentioned this to him earlier, maybe I wouldn't be lying here now.

Then, mercifully, everything turned black again.

***

I was waking up again, but knew better than to open my eyes. I lifted my lids just a tad to see if the stabbing pain would come back. So far, so good. I opened them a little more and saw a sea of faces in front of me: Mom, Detective Sterling, Lannie, Paula, Taylor, Thomas, P.J., and Derek. Tatters was sitting on my stomach staring into my face. I gave everyone a smile and gingerly tried to move my head. It wasn't too bad. It hurt, but it wasn't that searing pain I'd experienced before. It dawned on me that I was in the hospital, and that I could thank their wonder drugs for my comfort.

"Wow! It sure is good to see everybody." My throat was dry, so I pointed to the water bottle, and Mom lifted it to my lips. I smiled my thanks to her and looked at Tatters.

"My hero!"

My little boy actually grinned.

"How did you get Tatters in here? You know dogs aren't allowed."

Mom pointed to her shopping bag and put her fingers to her lips to remind Tatters to be quiet. "Nobody needs to know that he's here, and he promised to be very, very quiet."

"What time is it anyway?"

"It's four o'clock Friday afternoon. You've been asleep most of the day, and the doctors said that you have a serious bump on your head but that you will be back to normal in a day or two."

I lifted my hand to feel that my head was swathed in bandages. I had a moment of terror. "What about my hairdo?"

Mom patted my hand. "Your hair grows fast. They had to shave a teeny-weeny section to put in a few stitches."

Darn! And it looked so good.

Taylor moved closer to my bed and said, "Penny, I'll help you do your hair. Please don't worry."

171

That's my little sister!

Then I remembered my date today with Derek and Loretta and felt a stab of disappointment. "I'm sorry I missed our picnic. Can I have a raincheck? I really was looking forward to it."

"You bet, Penny." Derek winked at me, and I knew that our picnic would be one to remember. "Just get better, okay? You had us all very worried. I just about went out of my mind when I saw the emergency squad and the police cruisers at your shop in the middle of the night. Angela filled me in on what happened. I'm really glad you're going to be all right."

I gazed into his beautiful green eyes and knew that he meant every word he was saying.

I looked at Paula. "Where's Andy?"

"He's taking care of the store, and he told me to tell you that you had better be back soon. Penny, he is very concerned about you."

I turned toward Mom and asked, "Where's Alice?" I directed my next question to Detective Sterling. "Did you arrest Tony Delamar?"

There was an uncomfortable silence; nobody would make eye contact with me. Mom looked toward Detective Sterling for help.

"I had better answer that, Penny," he said. "No, we didn't arrest Tony Delamar."

"But then who…"

He held up his hand in that familiar gesture for silence. I wisely decided to let him tell his story.

The detective continued. "We knew about the Delamar-Walker connection from the Dayton police. It seems that Charley met Mr. Delamar in a bar and tried to recruit him into his drug business, but Mr. Delamar declined. He had had scrapes with the law in his younger days and wanted to go 'straight.' He moved to Columbus to be butler/chauffeur to his mother's best friend, Amelia Borden. Charley knew Mr. Delamar was in Columbus and approached him, in the same way he approached Emile Schwartz, to be his bodyguard. Charley threatened to tell Amelia Borden about Mr. Delamar's past, but Ms. Borden already knew about that."

So that's how he got the job. Now I understood the argument I overheard between the two of them the night of the dance.

"Well, if Tony didn't try to kill me, then who did?"

"I'm getting to that." Jack Sterling hesitated for a moment to gather his thoughts. "Penny, I'm sorry to have to tell you that Alice Dixon murdered Charley Walker and tried to kill you."

"No! No way! I don't believe that for a second."

Mom grabbed my hand, and I noticed the sadness in her eyes. "Penny, believe it. Everything that Detective Sterling is telling you is the truth, and we have proof."

"Proof? But Mom, Alice is your friend. She wouldn't hurt me."

Mom answered, "Penny, Alice left a letter that told the whole story. She explained what she did, and why she did it, before trying to take her own life."

"What? Alice is dead?"

Detective Sterling said, "No, she's not dead. We found her in time."

"How did she try to kill herself?"

"Alice took a bottle of sleeping pills. What your mom didn't tell you is that we first tried to call Alice for the key to Whimsies. We couldn't reach her on the phone, and that's when we called Paula and Andy. After the squad brought you to the hospital, I sent some officers to her house to see what was wrong. They found her near death, and also found a letter she had written that explained everything. It was on the nightstand next to her bed."

"That's unbelievable. I still don't know why she tried to kill me."

"Penny, Alice knew you were questioning people who knew Charley, and she feared that it was only a matter of time before you found out that she, too, had a motive."

I couldn't stop the tears from coming. P.J. appeared at my side and touched my cheek. "Pen, if it's any consolation, Alice was in so much emotional pain she didn't realize what she was doing."

"Bull!" exploded Lannie. "That's all a load of crap! Alice knew exactly what she was doing when she tried to kill Penelope. She's only sorry she got caught!"

Everyone was quiet for a time as we tried to reconcile the Alice we thought we all knew with Alice the murderer.

"Tell me what happened," I whispered.

"I'll tell you what we know." Detective Sterling got comfortable in a chair next to my bed and continued with his story. "Alice Dixon lived in Akron years ago. She was widowed at a young age when her only daughter, Maggie, was only ten-years old. It was hard for her to make ends meet on her husband's pension, so she took a nursing job at the Akron Community Hospital in the cancer ward."

"That must be how she came to run her hospice company here in Columbus," I interjected.

Detective Sterling nodded. "Maggie was a good kid and a good student by all accounts. When she was fifteen, she and her best friend, Sally Reid, went to a neighborhood party."

A light bulb went on in my head. "Would that be Bob's niece? You know, our mailman?"

"Yeah. Well, Alice was very protective of her daughter, and only let her go because the party was well-chaperoned. It seems that a couple of boys from the neighborhood crashed the party and convinced the girls to go for a ride with them. The boys had been drinking heavily."

"Don't tell me...one of the boys was Charley Walker." Everything was finally falling into place. "Lannie, did you know that Charley lived in Akron?"

"Yes, I knew he moved to Columbus while he was in high school, but I thought it was to be close to relatives after his father died."

Detective Sterling said, "That's partly true. Anyway, the kids did leave the party, and took the other boy's family car. That boy was also fifteen-years old, and had taken the car without his parents' knowledge. You can imagine how the tragedy occurred. The young man lost control of the car and ran into a light pole. The two girls were killed instantly, and the driver is spending the rest of his life in a wheelchair. Charley came out of the crash without a scratch. It was later learned that he was the one who supplied the liquor."

I couldn't imagine the pain and suffering of those poor families.

"What happened then?"

"Well, they say Charley's father died of a broken heart, although I think booze and cigarettes helped him along. Edna Walker moved to Columbus because she had grown up here and hoped that she and Charley could start a new life without the stigma of the accident."

Tatters started to get restless, so Mom picked him up and stuck him in her shopping bag.

"Penny darling, we have all heard the story, and I think it's time the rest of us clear out for awhile" — her glance took in most of my guests — "so you can hear the rest of the story. I'll be back in a couple of hours."

P.J., Paula, Derek, Taylor, and Thomas formed a line to parade by my bed and kiss my cheek. I was truly grateful to be alive and that my friends and family didn't have to suffer like the families of those poor kids.

"Do you want a little more agua before I leave, darling?"

"Yes, mamacita." I felt better knowing things were back to normal.

The only two remaining were Lannie and Jack Sterling. I looked at him and asked, "Do I have to keep calling you 'detective'?"

"By all means, no. Please call me Jack."

"Okay, Jack. Did Alice know that the Walkers had moved to Columbus?"

"No, all she knew was that they left town. Alice was in a state of deep depression after Maggie's death, and it took her a few years to get herself back together. She moved here when the hospice opportunity presented itself. An old friend of Alice's from her nursing days invited her into a partnership in the new business. Alice packed up her things, vowed to make a new life for herself, and never looked back. Her friends and colleagues never even knew she had a daughter."

"I can vouch for that... So why did she kill Charley after all these years?"

Lannie put her hand on Jack's shoulder and said, "I think I can answer that. Charley and I were divorced, and he had moved to Dayton by the time you went to work with Alice at Whimsies. She knew I was divorced from someone named Charley, but his name was rarely mentioned, certainly not by me, and Alice had completely put him out of her mind. Then, when he came back to town, everybody was talking about him. She must have realized that he was the same Charley Walker who had caused her daughter's death. Alice had this planned, Penelope."

"Why do you say that?"

"She took Max's wrench well before the murder and went to Charley's condo days later. She bashed him over the head — Jack was right, it was a crime of passion — and planted the wrench in Stella's garbage can." Lannie managed a devilish grin. "Alice knew how difficult Stella could be."

"That makes sense, Lannie, and I can even understand why she snapped and killed Charley...but why did she go after me?"

Jack answered this time. "According to her letter, she knew you were asking questions and was afraid you were going to ask her if she knew Charley. Alice didn't want to lie to you, Penny."

"She didn't want to lie to me, so she decided to kill me instead? That's ridiculous!" I thought about that for a minute. I guess her mind was pretty twisted by that point. It's just so hard to think of Alice doing something like that. "So Alice is the one who called me last night and told me there was a fire?"

Jack sighed. "Yeah... She knew you would run right over and check on your shop. She also knew you would check out the basement door, so she stood behind it and waited to strike."

"What did she hit me with?"

They both looked at each other, reluctant to answer.

"Well?" I persisted.

Lannie cleared her throat and muttered, "With your hammer... But she didn't break it."

"My beautiful Nieman Marcus hand-painted porcelain hammer?"

Lannie nodded. "The very one."

Jack added, "If Alice had used anything more substantial, you probably wouldn't be here now."

That was a sobering thought. I was going to treat my tools with even more reverence than usual in the future.

Lannie thought for a moment and said, "I guess Alice pushed you down the stairs, followed you down when you fell forward, and decided to tie you up and leave you to...you know..."

Yeah, I know. I am so grateful that they found me. I vowed to give Tatters a whole bag of treats when I got out of the hospital, and I blessed my mother's "radar" yet again. I was so happy to be alive and have such a wonderful family and such good friends that I started to cry.

Jack looked uncomfortable and said, "Maybe we'd better go now, Lannie, and let Penny get some rest."

I agreed that that was a good idea. Lannie gave me a gentle hug and Detective — no, Jack — patted my cheek. I closed my eyes and started to doze off. I could hear rustling in the room and peeked out from under my lashes. Jack and Lannie were standing at the foot of my bed in a heated embrace. They were whispering, but I could make out the words.

"You know, beautiful, I could get used to holding you like this for, say, the next hundred years or so."

"No way, buster. You're either in this for the long haul or not all!"

That's my Lannie. I fell asleep happy.

Chapter 13

The bright light galvanized them into action. Kevin and Miranda both jumped behind the stairway and waited for the footsteps that signaled their attacker was descending. One...two...almost close enough to grab a foot. Kevin reached out and grabbed a heavy work boot. "Now, Miranda! Grab the other foot." The big man made a terrible noise as he tumbled the remaining distance to the bottom of the stairs, breaking his neck in the fall.

Tatters was standing on my foot. "Move away, Tatters. I promise I'm not going anywhere."

I was propped up against the counter at Whimsies with my laptop next to the cash register. My mojo was working for me, and the book would be finished in no time. Ever since my brush with death, Tatters refused to be more than an inch away from me. I was thinking of getting him some therapy if this went on much longer.

I had a steady stream of visitors all morning. My friends and family had all come to the shop to see with their own eyes that I was okay and to commiserate with me about Alice. My fellow shopkeepers offered to help me with anything I needed. Emile came by to check on my hair and deemed that he could fix me up during my lunch break. I still had two little stitches in my head, but the swelling had gone down appreciably.

Grace was in my office, finishing up the invoices for me. She told me she would be thrilled to work with me at Whimsies and be my new partner. Alice, in a gesture of contrition, had given me her half of the store. Alice pled guilty to murder and attempted murder and will be spending the rest of her life behind bars. What a waste!

Derek spent an hour here this morning, just hanging out and being good company for me. He offered to let his two most-prized workers come over if I needed a break. I declined, saying that I still had Paula and Andy, and that Grace would be spending several hours a week in the shop, now that Lily was soon to start at the Goddard School. I felt emotionally full to have such wonderful people to look after me.

The front door jangled, and I looked up to see Stella peeking into the shop. Her bruises were mostly gone by now, and she looked stunning in a navy blue sundress and a white straw hat with a navy ribbon. I could tell that she was nervous about approaching me.

"Come on in, Stella. It's nice of you to drop by."

She visibly relaxed and clickety-clicked up to the counter. "Penny, I just wanted to let you know…that is…I'm sorry about all that stuff with Alice."

Wow. Stella was being a decent human being, and I wondered how long this would last.

"Even if you were mean to me" — not long I guess — "you didn't deserve to be almost killed."

"Why, thank you, Stella. I appreciate your concern. And since you were so nice to come over and see me, I'd like to offer you a little gift as a token of my gratitude."

"Oh, how nice, Penny. And how unlike you."

"Just a minute while I get the stepladder from the back…"